The Chosen Historian
Evin Driscol Series

Randi Ertz

TLT Publishing

Chicago

THE LITTLE THINGS PUBLISHING, LLC

Chicago, Illinois

Copyright © 2010 Randi Ertz.

Printed in the United States of America

Cover Design by Michael C. Ludwig
Book Design by Cameron Ruen
Edited by Meredith Carey
Published by The Little Things (TLT) Publishing, LLC

The Little Things (TLT) Publishing, LLC
Chicago, Illinois
tltpublishing.com

ISBN: 978-0-9844013-0-7

First Paperback Edition: May 2010

[1. Vampires-fiction 2. Supernatural-fiction 3. Chicago-fiction]
I. Title II. Series III. Randi Ertz

I dedicate this book to two very important people. To my grandmother Noami who I miss dearly and think of often, and Alphera who was taken to young and will be missed by her family and friends. You both are always in my prayers.

ACKNOWLEDGMENT

I have several people to thank who helped make this book possible. To my amazing editor, Meredith Carey, who did an amazing job editing - even though I probably drove her to insanity throughout the project. To my illustrator, Michael Ludwig, who understood my vision for the book and produced an amazing cover. To my wonderful partner, Cameron Ruen, who has supported me throughout this adventure and designed the book. Last, but not least, to Elli, who convinced me to read my first vampire book. Thanks to her, I have become obsessed with all things supernatural.

The Chosen Historian
Evin Driscol Series

 PROLOGUE

WE all wish we could change something in our past, and I am no different. For some, it's a kiss that never happened, or a choice they made that they wish they could take back. For me, it's both of those things and more. I am one hundred and seventy-one years old. I have lived through the Civil War, WWI, WWII, the Korean War, the Vietnam War, and the Persian Gulf War. I have outlived most of my immediate family members. I have seen slavery abolished, seen Americans struggle through the Great Depression, and seen Martin Luther King Jr. give his "I Have a Dream" speech during the Civil Rights Movement. I enjoyed the free love of the 60s and 70s. I witnessed the birth of MTV and watched the world become mesmerized by the glamorous 80s—glam metal hairdos, punk rockers, and colorful clothing. Then in the 90s came Generation X with their grunge music (or hip-hop, whatever you preferred), the wonderful worldwide web known as the Internet, and globalization, all of which I lived through. And now I'm presently coasting through the new millennium of Generation Y—lazy, self-indulgent geniuses who want to use technology as a way to continue to be lazy while they try to cure the world of all the problems the generations before them left behind. Personally, I think it's great that humanity is finally starting to realize they need to do something about how shitty the world has become on their watch. In a way, I care even more than they do, because I plan on living for the rest of eternity. If these damn humans keep destroying the planet, well then, I'm screwed too, am I not?

My name is Evin Driscol and I am a Daywalker. While I'm glad I've had the chance to see all these changes, for better or for worse, I do have a few regrets. I regret voting for Reagan. I regret not telling Marianne Winthrop that I loved her. But most of all, I regret not going back to see my mother after becoming a Daywalker. I never knew what happened to my mother and my three younger siblings. I always wondered what happened to my family after I left them in 1865, when women had little to no rights and my family was struggling to run my father's shoe shop after he died.

As for Marianne, well, she was my sweetheart growing up. When I left for the Civil War, I believed I may not come back, and at the time, I thought I was doing the right thing by not telling her that I loved her. I thought, that way, if I didn't come back, it would be easier for her to move on. She wrote me all the time. I wrote her when I got the chance, but as time went by, I stopped writing, consumed by my internal struggle with the death all around me. Today's wars are bad enough, but let me tell you, they don't hold a candle to the gruesomeness and violence of the wars of past eras, when there was no modern medicine as we know it now. Anyway, when I stopped writing, Marianne naturally thought I'd been killed. Years later I found out she'd gone on to marry a successful businessman, an executive at a huge department store in Chicago.

I saw Marianne once in Chicago. It was 1875, years after the war was over, and I passed her walking down State Street one afternoon. I recognized her right away, though she was now in her early thirties. Our eyes met for a moment as we passed on the muddy road. She was being led by her husband, and I was being led by my instinct for the thirst. We had passed so close to each other I could have reached out and touched her. To this day, I still believe she recognized me, though I still looked almost as young as I did in my early twenties when she'd last seen me. I always wondered what she thought the moment our eyes met. All those years she thought I was dead . . . did she still think I was dead, that I was a figment of her imagination? Or did she really know it was me?

Of course, don't let me lead you to believe that I think of this often, because I don't. It's just a good way to start my story. I was born in 1841 in a small town in Iowa called Burlington. My parents, Shannon and Maureen Driscol, had five children: Ellison, me, Conor, Molly and Noami. My father Shannon Driscol was a hardworking Irishman whose family came from Wicklow, Ireland. He was an apprentice shoemaker in Dublin for many years before paying twenty American dollars to come here to the Land of Opportunity. My father settled in Burlington when he was twenty-eight years old and married my mother, Maureen. Although he was only a poor shoemaker, he loved his family and was an upstanding, well-respected man in our community. My mother's family was of half Irish and half German descent, and were farmers in a small town called Mediapolis, about thirty miles north of Burlington.

I'm only giving a little background about my family and myself because I think it's important to explain my life before my rebirth.

My sister Ellison, who everyone called Elli, was a few years older than me. In 1852, I was twelve years old and Elli was eighteen. My parents had wanted Elli to get an education, which was extremely rare for women at that time, because my father believed that my sister had the potential to be a great woman, much more than a small-town wife. Elli thought so, too. She was very, very intelligent. But she was also a romantic, and before our father could ship her off to school, she came home one evening and announced to the whole family that she was in love. She wanted to marry a man she had met named Shawn Kelley. He was from Chicago, and was in Burlington only briefly in order to conduct some business with the railroad, in which he had invested a significant sum of money. My father was furious. He had met Shawn once before, but had no idea he was courting my sister. Father refused to listen to Elli, and insisted she end things with Shawn, telling her that education was her future, and that family would come later (my dad couldn't have known how far ahead of his time he was in this sentiment). Elli ran out of the house crying that evening and never came back. My father contacted the Burlington Police first thing the following morning and reported Elli missing. A frantic investigation ensued, but no trace of Elli could be found. It was strange—no one that was questioned had ever heard of Shawn. It was as if he never existed. I was never sure if my father thought she was dead or if he believed she just ran away. My mother continued to take care of the home as if nothing had changed, though I would hear her crying at night.

My father was already a whiskey drinker, but he began to drink even more heavily after Elli disappeared. On April 21, 1858, Elli's birthday, my father had a few too many drinks at the local pub. He had become a big man over the years, with a big thirst, and, stumbling along the banks of the Mississippi on his way home, my father fell into the river and drowned. It had been raining that night, and the current was strong; between his size and his drunkenness, he was unable to pull himself up out of the water. After that, I became the man of the house at the age of sixteen, helping my mom run the shoe shop. We hired a man named Paul Gerst as our shoemaker, an easy fellow to work with, and a perfect and wonderful gentleman to my mother.

As I mentioned earlier, it was around this time that I also fell in love with a girl named Marianne Winthrop. We had gone to school together until I had to drop out to help my mother run the shop. Even after I left school, Marianne and I would take long walks along the riverfront, and she would read me novels under the apple tree outside her family's farm. Marianne was tall, with long, wild blond hair and sparkling blue eyes. We were complete opposites in almost every way. I had golden brown hair that always looked messy and brown eyes that would go hazel depending on my mood. My family was poor and ran a small shoe shop mending shoes, while her family owned a huge farm with hired help. Her father was also President of the local bank. Her parents never approved of me, saying that my father was a drunk and had left my family to fend for ourselves. However, we continued sneaking off to see each other as often as we could.

In 1860, Abraham Lincoln was voted President of the United States, and the following year the Civil War had begun. My mother was worried that I would be anxious to join the Union, which I was, but I didn't enlist until August 3, 1862, my twenty-first birthday. I loved my mother and my younger siblings, but I believed I had a higher purpose than running my father's shop. I knew that Paul would look out for my mother and my siblings. He had become a close friend to my mother, and he treated my siblings like they were his own children.

Marianne was distraught when I told her I was going off to Springfield, Illinois to join the ranks under Grant. I promised her I would come back for her when the war was over. I regret now that I lied to her, though not intentionally. Most of all, I regret that I never told her I loved her.

After joining the Union Army I realized that although I believed in Lincoln, and believed with all my heart that all men should be free, war was not something I ever wanted to see again. I barely survived the Civil War. I saw many men killed, and I killed many men. I was stabbed by a bayonet in my right leg at the battle of Petersburg, and without any kind of sanitary medical conditions as we know them today, I became very ill with fever. To have survived not only the battles, but the hunger, the cold, the diseases, the loneliness—all I can say about it now is that was surreal. In any event, I left Burlington a boy and came back home a man. I was twenty-four years old, grateful to have survived, and ready to settle down with my sweetheart, run my father's shoe shop, and take care of my family.

When I arrived home my mother looked tired and considerably older. Paul was still working at the shoe shop and was a gentleman in every way, doing everything he could to help my mother during my absence. My brother Conor had grown in to a huge man, much like our father, and was now twenty years old and married to a nice young woman. Conor ran the shoe shop, and Paul had taught him how to make and fix shoes. Molly was eighteen years old by this time. She would help our mother with the house and the shop during the day, and was taking classes at night. She also had a sweetheart. He did not come from a wealthy family (we were far from wealth ourselves), but he was a hard worker on his family's farm and wanted to marry Molly. My little sister Noami had grown to become a beautiful woman at the age of sixteen. Noami was the smartest girl I had ever met. She loved poetry and books, loved to learn, and wanted to go to a University when she turned eighteen years old to become a teacher. She talked of traveling around the world to places like Italy, Germany, France, Ireland, and even Asia. Noami was not only quick as a whip, but she was also able to attract the attention of young men everywhere she went. She had dark hair with golden-brown eyes and olive skin. She knew the boys in town noticed her, but she paid them no attention except to tease them every now again. She knew she didn't want to stay in Burlington. She wanted to explore the world.

You must be asking yourself what happened to Marianne. Well . . . when I came home, she was no longer in Burlington. My mother told me that when Marianne stopped hearing from me, she had given in to her parents and married a promising man who had landed an executive job with a huge department store in Chicago.

I tried to move on. I helped my brother in the shoe shop, but I felt like I was barging in on his work space. He loved to work in the shop, just like our father. I wondered whether I was meant to stay in Burlington or see the world myself, like Noami, but I knew I had to do something first before I did anything else, and that was to see Marianne. It was a ridiculous idea, I'll admit. But I was in love, and thinking of her is what had gotten me through the war. I lingered for several months in Burlington, and on

Christmas Eve, I told my family that I was leaving the following day. I told Conor that the shoe shop was his, that it always had been, and that he would do a far better job running it then I ever could. All that I asked was that he look after our mother and sisters. I knew he appreciated that I recognized all that he had done while I was away, and that I trusted him to be the man of the house. Molly was so wrapped up in her relationship that I doubt she even noticed me gone, and Noami said farewell, but she believed she would see me again. Noami had big plans to set out on her own for a University and to see the world, so she understood me not wanting to stay. My mother took it the hardest. She had just gotten me back, and now I was leaving again. I remember the chilly night in front of the fireplace when I told them all I was leaving. After everyone had gone to bed, my mother sat up in her rocking chair, her eyes beginning to tear up. Now, I had heard my mother cry before when my sister Elli disappeared, but I had never actually seen her cry, not even when I went off to war. I remember our conversation like it was yesterday.

"Evin, you were always my beautiful boy and I knew

you would become a wonderful man. Life has not been easy for you, but I want you to know that I love you with all my heart. I feel..."

"Mother, don't. I will be back," I assured her.

"No. Listen to me, Evin. I don't think you will come back this time. I don't know how I know this, but I do, and there is something I have to tell you. I always knew that Conor and Molly would stay here and continue on with the business and raise their families. But you, Elli, and Noami . . . you all were different, are different. Promise me that you will not change who you are, that you will always be my loving son with the gift of loving life. When you go to Chicago, I want you to look for Elli. I have never once believed she was dead. I want you to look for her, Evin. The three of you have special gifts that you do not know you possess. When you find your sister, I want the three of you to go to Ireland to meet your family. They will explain your gifts."

I never asked her to elaborate, but I knew I would do as she requested. I would find Elli, and go with her and Noami to Ireland to see our relatives and ask about our special gifts.

That was my last conversation with my mother.

⁓ Chapter 1 ⁓

"HEY there, handsome, give me a New Year's Eve kiss." The fiery redhead with green eyes reached up and grabbed my face with both hands and pressed her soft, warm lips against mine. I had never been kissed like that, but if a random woman *was* going to kiss me like that, it would only happen at Finnegan's Wake, a notoriously wild pub on Adams Street in the heart of Chicago.

I had just arrived in Chicago the night before and was lodging with James Allen, a friend who served with me in the Civil War. James worked at Finnegan's Wake as a bartender and bouncer and stayed in one of the apartments above.

It took me close to three days to get from Burlington to Chicago on horseback, though for humans now it would only take three and a half hours by train, and me about two hours at my top speed on foot. Anyway, I had arrived just in time for New Year's Eve. That evening, I considered spending the night with the redhead in the pub, knowing she would probably be more than willing to go home with me. I didn't have to love her, nor her me; I know it sounds horrible, being that I was in Chicago to look for Marianne. But, as I constantly had to remind myself, she was married to someone else now. I had no hopes of Marianne leaving her husband. I was only there to tell her how I felt.

While I flirted with the fiery redhead, I noticed a woman in the back of the dark smoky bar gambling with several men. The woman looked confident and defiant, like nothing could stop her. She had a strong laugh and a vibrant voice, and I found myself staring at her. I couldn't tell why, but she looked so familiar—although she was all the way at the other end of the pub, I could have sworn it was my sister Elli.

I could never forget what my sister looked like, every detail, because she looked so much like me. Elli was about five foot seven compared to my height of six feet, and she had my golden brown hair and golden brown eyes that changed to hazel when we were excited. Of course, her hair was much longer than mine, hanging past her shoulders. She was slim, but with womanly curves. The woman in the bar could have been Elli's identical twin, except for one thing—she didn't look any older than when I had seen her last. She still looked as if she was eighteen or nineteen years old, but Elli would have been thirty by now.

"I'll be back," I mumbled to the fiery redhead.

"Okay," she said playfully, "but don't leave, darling, because I'm hoping we can leave together and have our own little good time."

"Yeah, okay," I mumbled again as I stood up and made my way through the packed, noisy pub, but before I could get to her, the woman who looked like Elli stood up suddenly, raked in all her money, and turned and made her way out the back door. I was seconds behind her, quickly pushing open the door that led out to a dark alley filled with trash and snow. I looked around, but she was gone. How could that be? I had only been seconds behind her. I ran through the alley leading out onto Adams Street. It was freezing outside, but the streets were crowded with people nonetheless, New Year's Eve revelers spilling out of the many bars up and down the street, yelling and dancing.

I quickly scanned the crowd for Elli's mysterious twin, and caught a glimpse of her turning the corner onto Clark Street. I picked up my pace in order to catch up, following her for several blocks until I was completely unsure of where I was. She turned into another dark alley, and when I followed, I saw her enter a door with an "Exit" sign hanging above it. As I made my way to the door, I heard footsteps behind me and turned to see three men sauntering down the dark alley towards me. This was not going to be good.

One of the men was about five foot eleven, with black hair that fell down around his shoulders and pale skin. He wore an expensive-looking gentleman's suit and spoke with a strong accent.

"Why are you following the young lady, my friend?"

He began to walk around the left side of me, while another man with shaggy blond hair and greenish-gray eyes, also very pale-skinned, circled around my other side.

"I thought that I might know the young lady and was trying to catch up with her. I was hoping to speak with her," I replied, with more concern in my voice than I usually liked to show.

"You do *not* know her," the same man responded sharply, with what I now recognized as an Eastern European accent.

"Do you know her, sir?" I asked, trying to sound unflustered. "If so, maybe you can help me figure out if I actually do." I realized that instead of sounding conversational, I sounded challenging and defiant. I noticed the blond-haired man was now extremely close to me on the other side, while the third man stood back and watched what was playing out. "I don't want any trouble, I just wanted to—"

"To what?" he interrupted me. "Make a new friend? Enjoy the company of a woman tonight?" He paused for a moment while he and the blond man continued to circle me. Then, in a condescending tone, he said, "Well, that is just too bad."

I then felt the blond man jump on me from behind so quickly I had no time to react. He knocked me forward onto the ground, dug his fingernails into my arms as he held me down, and then he bit down on my neck. I was in shock. I had braced myself for a fight the moment I saw them coming towards me in the alley, but this was totally unexpected. What was happening? What the hell was this all about? Who *were* these people? I felt another set of hands on me, and another bite on my arm. I felt a strange, cold sensation all over, then realized with horror—they were sucking the blood out of me! I couldn't move. I felt paralyzed, and even if I could have moved, they were holding me so tight it would have been useless. I tried to speak, to beg, but no words would come out of my mouth. They were going to kill me. They were going to suck the life right out of me. I could feel the ground against my face, muddy and hard below the wet layer of dirty snow. I closed my eyes and waited for death to come upon me. I couldn't believe I had made it through the war only to be senselessly murdered by these lunatics attacking me—feeding off of me?—in a dark alley.

Then I heard a woman's voice. I tried to open my eyes to see where the voice was coming from. My vision was hazy, but I could see the same young woman, the one I had been following, standing over me.

"Stop! You're killing him! Stop! He's my brother!" she screamed. The men released me and she dropped to her knees next to me. "Evin! Evin, stay with me. Don't die. I won't let you die."

She was trying to sound reassuring, but I could hear the fear in her voice. I knew I was on the brink of death.

"We didn't know he was your brother. We saw him following you out of the pub and we thought we would have some fun with him," said the blond-haired man.

"We didn't know, Elli." This was a new voice to me, a kinder voice, and I realized it must be the voice of the man who had been watching from a distance, who hadn't participated in the attack.

"Shawn, we do not play when we hunt. Who are we to condemn men before we know whether they should be condemned? " she demanded angrily. She held my head up, focusing intently on my face. "Evin, you must listen to me or you will die. You must do exactly as I tell you. Do you understand?" she asked, her voice now quieter, soothing me.

"I understand." I struggled to respond, my voice barely audible.

"You must drink from me, Evin." She put her wrist to her mouth, and I saw sharp incisor-like teeth I had never seen before. She broke open the skin and held her wrist to my mouth, saying, "Drink, Evin." So I drank. At first, I swallowed only a little—I was so weak that was all I could do. But as the blood flowed into me, I began to feel my strength returning. Her blood tasted sweet, not at all salty and metallic like I had expected, and I began to crave it. I grabbed her arm and began to suck more and more. I don't know how long I drank my sister's blood, but it was long enough to make her weak. When she whispered, "Evin, that's enough," I let her go.

This is how I became a vampire. To the supernatural world, I became known as a Daywalker, like my sister Elli.

⌒⟳ Chapter 2 ⟲⌒

TO describe the hundred and forty-six years after my rebirth on January 1, 1866 would take volumes. But if you want to know about those moments of my life (and I mean it when I call those years "moments," because I'm going to live forever), you will have to look for them in the other books I've written; here, there is only time to briefly describe what happened next.

Elli took me to their home, an old house with a deep, secure basement on Halsted Avenue. She explained to me what they were . . . vampires. The word sounded new to my ears, as if I had never heard it before; however, there they were, the figures of legends and nightmares, right there in the flesh . . . my own flesh. Though I still felt extremely on-edge with the two vampires who attacked me, I also knew that at this point, I was changed. Elli explained to me that they were a coven.

Sebastian Markic, the one with the shoulder length dark hair and the Slavic accent, was the oldest. Sebastian was from Croatia and was turned in 1402 when he was twenty-eight years old. Elli told me they considered him the leader of the coven, although I would come to learn he was not a strict leader and did not demand that anyone stay within the coven. However, Sebastian had quite a temper, which flared up most severely when he did not understand something and had to rely on others to explain. He was fiercely independent and hated showing signs of weakness.

The blond man with the striking greenish-gray eyes was the son of a Spanish infanta and a German warlord. His name was Niklas Urz. Niklas had been a sailor, and had sailed with Christopher Columbus on his second trip to the new territories in 1493 when he landed on Marie-Galante.

When Niklas returned to Spain in 1502, he met Sebastian, and they became lovers. He was turned by Sebastian in 1502 when he was twenty-one years old. Niklas was flamboyant and mischievous. He loved to drink blood, even more so then the rest of us, and had no problem taking more than "just a little" from his victims.

The third man's name was Shawn Kelley. He was the man my sister had run away with. Shawn was about six foot two, which was exceptionally tall for the time. He was a businessman of sorts, was good with money, and was a gentleman in almost every way . . . except that he drank people's blood now. He came from a prominent New York family and met Sebastian in 1850 when he was twenty-two years old. Sebastian lured him into the vampire world and turned him because he was smart and Sebastian needed him. Sebastian and Niklas had not yet been able to carve out a comfortable enough living for themselves on their own, and needed a practical fellow like Shawn to make sure their needs were met. Shawn stayed with Niklas and Sebastian for two years, helping them establish a home in Chicago, and was then allowed to venture out on his own. This, Elli told me, is when he met her in Burlington. He had invested in the railroad there, and was visiting on business when he saw her walking on the riverfront. As striking and graceful as she was, it's no surprise that he fell in love with her instantly. He remained in Burlington, and after months of secretly courting her, Shawn confided to Elli that he was no ordinary man. He told her he was a vampire, and promised he would never hurt her. Elli told me she had been a little shocked by this, but that she had already sensed Shawn was different somehow. She knew he was a good man and that he would never hurt her, and, most importantly, she knew she was in love and that Shawn was her soul mate. When our father refused to meet Shawn formally and give his blessing, she decided to run away with him. She asked him to turn her so she could be with him forever, and he did, on her nineteenth birthday. They had come to Chicago together, where they had been living as a coven with Sebastian and Niklas ever since.

Elli's story surprised me much less than I expected. Of course, this would usually have been a lot for anyone to take in. But I was not just anyone. Not anymore. When you are reborn, your senses become altered and enhanced; you find yourself much more powerful and agile than you were before. The unknown no longer frightens you. Your curiosity becomes insatiable, and you want to explore everything.

Elli told me that she and I were not the same as Shawn, Sebastian and Niklas, because they were true vampires—they had to sleep during the day and stay out of the sun. Soon after she was turned, Elli had noticed she did not become weak and fatigued just before sunrise like the others, so, always headstrong and daring, she tempted fate and stepped into the sun. She discovered that the sun had no effect on her, and realized she could not only walk in the sun but could also go long periods of time without drinking blood. Sebastian had told her he had never heard of a vampire that could do this, and that when he had tried to step into the daylight when he was first turned, his skin had begun to burn. Elli thought that because we were of the same blood, I would also be able to walk in the sun and to go without feeding for long periods of time. As we soon discovered, she was right. Word about us spread quickly through the vampire underworld, and Elli and I became known as Daywalkers, vampires who could walk in the sun and feed very little. We also could hold color in our skin, where the others turned pale over time, making us less conspicuous in the human world.

Over the next decade, Shawn, Elli and I stayed in Chicago with Sebastian and Niklas. Shawn helped establish Sebastian and Niklas financially as well as ourselves. The three of us were inseparable, and we were not so unlike ordinary people. We went out on the town at night, enjoying the pubs, clubs and theatres. We read the papers and talked about politics. We did not like to drink blood. Well, I shouldn't say we didn't like it, because that's not true. Naturally, we loved it. What we didn't like was to kill for the blood. We learned to take only what we needed from those we chose; usually they woke up weak and light-headed, not remembering the night before.

During the day when Shawn slept, Elli and I would enjoy the parks, watch the tourists, and shop. Of course, we needed sleep as well, but not like the others. We could go days without sleeping, and when we did sleep, we only slept for short periods of time.

Eventually we began to tire of Sebastian and Niklas and their old-fashioned ways. We realized we wanted to see the world. We decided in 1875 to leave not only Chicago but Sebastian and Niklas. Sebastian had said he would never force us to stay, so we told him about our plans to leave. I could tell he was sad about this, because we were the ones who kept him in touch with the human world, but his only request was that we make sure his expenses were in order, and Shawn did just that. Niklas was upset that we were allowed to leave, and even threw a fit, but I think he was also relieved we were going because we tended to squash his fun playing with his victims. Niklas not only liked to torment his victims, but to kill them as well, which we did not approve of. Sebastian was always torn on this issue. His heart was not in playing games or killing, though he could kill easily enough; but he always felt the need to make Niklas happy.

The day we planned to leave, Elli and I went shopping on State Street, her favorite pastime. As we walked out of Marshall Field's, I saw a woman I immediately recognized.

Marianne.

She was older, in her early thirties now, but still very beautiful. She was walking alongside a man, her arm intertwined in his. The man looked to be a few years older than she was, and I knew it had to be her husband. She looked so happy. So many memories came flashing back—I suddenly remembered why I had originally come to Chicago: to tell her how much I loved her. I wanted to run to her, to tell her everything, but I knew I couldn't.

Marianne and her husband came walking up the street towards Elli and me. I was frozen in place on the street in the sunlight, not breathing. We technically do not need to breathe, and still do it more out of habit than anything else; but that wasn't why I had stopped this time. The sight of Marianne made my breath catch in my throat . . . just like a human. People were starting to notice my strange behavior. Elli noticed, too, but continued nonchalantly window-shopping, pulling me along the street behind her. As Marianne and I passed each other, our eyes met for a few seconds—a few seconds that felt like an eternity, even to me, and I swear I saw her bright smile darken almost imperceptibly and a hint of sadness enter her sparkling blue eyes.

Did she recognize me? Or did she think I was a figment of her imagination? Even today, I still look twenty-four years old, ten years younger than I would have been in her mind that day; after all, she had last seen me when I was twenty-one. After we passed one another, Marianne continued to look forward, chattering with her husband as they walked. She never looked back. I kept looking until I could no longer see her or hear her.

Which was a long, long time. Our hearing is exceptional.

After that I knew I was ready to get out of Chicago. I did not want to see Marianne again. What good would that do? That was my old life.

When Elli and I got home, our stuff was already packed, and we waited for Shawn to wake so we could leave. Sebastian was an early riser, and he said his good-byes to us. When Shawn woke we headed for the train station, our suitcases filled with nothing but memories of our past lives and some clothes. We didn't need anything else. Shawn's business sense ensured our financial stability would grow over time, due to the good investments he had made for us.

Over the next century and half, the three of us explored the world. We traveled throughout most of Europe, stopping in England, but for some reason never venturing into Ireland, the land of our ancestors. We traveled through Morocco, Libya, and Egypt, exploring the Great Pyramids. We ventured through the Holy Land, the Middle East, and made our way through China, Thailand, and Indonesia; then to New Guinea, Australia and New Zealand and back up to see parts of Japan before crossing the Pacific back to America. We then traveled through South America, seeing the Amazon River and Angel Falls in Venezuela, and relaxing in Aruba and Barbados. Shawn loved the Virgin Islands, so we stayed there a while. The difficulty of living on an island, for a vampire, is that you must sleep during the day, and it's hard to find adequate cover. But vampires are not exactly what you think. We don't have to sleep in a coffin, though some prefer the light-tight space. Shawn preferred a dark room, just like a human. He had the luxury of security when he slept because we were always near, and the two of us could sleep whenever we felt like it.

It was hard for Shawn, who at first had to feed every night, when we would go on long walkabouts (a term I adopted after spending time with the Aborigines in Australia) where there would be no humans around. But after all the time we spent in the wild, he learned to make do with feeding on animals, and eventually, he grew to prefer it. Shawn also learned to go longer stretches of time, almost a month, without feeding, just like us. It wasn't as easy for him as it was for us, and he had to train himself, whereas we had always been that way, from the day we were reborn.

We then came back to North America and traveled throughout the States. You would think that over a hundred years would be long enough to see everything, but it's not. Even now, at a hundred and seventy-one years old, I have yet to see everything.

We met a lot of supernatural beings during our travels that Sebastian had never told us about, either because chose not to, or because he didn't know about them himself. We met other vampires—but no other Daywalkers, of course—living all over the world. As the years went by, vampires began to organize, much like ordinary humans. By the 1920s, a Vampire Federation had been established, with presidents representing each country, governors over the different territories, and lieutenants who enforced vampire law.

Before the Vampire Federation (VF), what we now call vampire law had been followed for centuries without actually being spelled out, though it was enforced by the elders. However, the population of vampires had grown so much over time that the majority of the elder vampires felt these rules needed to be established for us all and be enforced by an organization. Breaking the law was a serious matter, and governors and lieutenants in your area determined the severity of your punishment based on which law you had broken.

I guess I should tell you what the laws are, or at least the major ones. They are fairly simple. There used to be six major rules: One, always obey your sire. Two, if you turn a human, you are responsible for that new vampire. Three, you must never kill another vampire (unless your President grants you permission, an amendment made in the 1920s). Four, you must never turn a child. Five, you must follow human law as closely as possible. Six, you must not let the human world know of our kind.

This last law has since been removed, because the VF announced our existence to the world several years ago. Many vampires were outraged at being "outed" to the world, but the VF is headed by the underworld's top vampire leaders, known as the elders, and all vampires are required to obey. The VF's top scientists had developed a synthetic blood substitute that tasted almost identical to human blood and provided the same nutrients, and the elders believed that with this, we could co-exist with the human population. In other words, it was finally safe for us to come out of the shadows, so to speak. A new law was added just before coming out to the world, which is that vampires are strictly forbidden from killing humans. We can drink from a human if the human is willing, but never by force. This eliminated the chase, and really pissed a lot of vampires off.

Shawn, Elli, and I were relieved that we no longer had to hide. Shawn did not like the taste of the synthetic blood, but he didn't like to drink from humans, either. Elli and I had no problem with the synthetic blood and were glad we no longer had to scrounge for human scum to feed off of, though we did still crave human blood from time to time. And there were other alternatives now as well. Always opportunistic, humans began selling blood drained from animals during the meat-packing process to vampires. Of course, it was not as good as human blood, but some vampires thought it was better than synthetic.

I mentioned that we ran into other supernaturals on our walkabout of the world; skin-walkers and shapeshifters, werewolves, witches, fairies, piskies, and many other creatures. We also heard of elves, said to be angelic creatures that were similar to fairies. I could talk for hours about the supernatural world and those I have met, but that is another story in itself. I will say that we vampires were the first to come out, then witches and wiccans, and then werewolves; but not all supernaturals are out. Fairies only live in this world on a part-time basis, and tend to live most of their lives in Seelie or Unseelie Court. We don't know much about shapeshifters except that they don't want anyone to know a lot about them, and as far as angelic creatures, well, they are only hearsay. No one has ever been able to say for sure that they exist except for fairies, and they refuse to discuss the topic.

Now that I have told you about my human life, my rebirth, and my travels around the globe with Elli and Shawn, it comes time for me to move forward to the present.

THE CHOSEN HISTORIAN

⟳ Chapter 3 ⟲

"EVIN, wake up! You're going to be late for your lecture,"
Elli yelled up the stairs, and I instantly opened my eyes.
I have never understood why she feels the need to even
speak to me sometimes, because we have the unique gift of
hearing each other's thoughts if we're in a certain radius of
each other. Whenever I mention this in my thoughts, she
always replies out loud, "Because we want to be as normal
as we can, don't we?" Of course, if you were a third party
present for this conversation, you would be highly confused
as to why only Elli was talking, though Shawn was used to
it by now.

I thought, *I'll be down in a minute*, knowing she would hear me.

I turned my attention towards the fuzzy ball of fur lying next to me. "It's time to get up, Maiko." Maiko was my dog, a black and tan Shiba Inu with a little red on the top of her head, around her ears, paws and her fox-like tail. Her breed is known to be one of the smartest dogs in the world, a Japanese breed said to have originated from the fox. I found her in Kyoto after a vampire had sucked her almost dry, with just an ounce of life left in her. She was just so damn cute and sad-looking lying on the muddy ground that I gave her some of my blood and made her into my eternal best friend.

Maiko instantly sat up when I spoke to her and licked my face. Though we slept, we did not sleep like others of our kind, and we did not sleep like humans. I am completely aware of my surroundings when I sleep.

Maiko jumped off the bed and moved with lightning speed downstairs to our big kitchen. I followed milliseconds behind her. I sat down on a stool across from my sister, who was cutting up food—that is, normal food that humans eat—on the island in the center or the room. We have no reason to eat food to survive, though we can still taste the flavors. All we need to survive is blood.

"Why are you cooking food? It smells good but—" Then I saw Elli smile, and I knew she was up to something fishy. "Who's coming over, Elli? I'm in no mood for company."

I walked to the bar and poured myself a glass of Bloody Paddy (Synthetic) Whiskey while Elli poured some Canine Fury (also synthetic) for Maiko.

"Evin, you need to relax and socialize more. You might even meet a nice girl someday." Elli paused. "The girl who's coming over is no one you know. She's in my art class. She's interested in going to your lecture with me."

"Well, you'll have to meet me there. I'm meeting with Professor Jordan before the lecture," I lied. Elli was always trying to set me up with girls. While it was true that I hadn't dated anyone seriously since . . . well, since Marianne, I hated set-ups. Awkward.

Shawn walked in on the conversation and chimed in. "Elli, you shouldn't pressure Evin so much. When he's ready to meet someone, he will." Shawn tucked his paper under his arm and sat down on a stool at the counter.

Let me explain a little about Shawn. He had become a prominent businessman by this time, and had made all of us very financially well-off. He loves to smoke cigars, reads voraciously, and plays golf (by moonlight, of course). He's an honest man and consults for the VF governor of Illinois.

Elli, however, is another story. She still has a wild side, though it's been tamed down somewhat because of her love for Shawn. Her hair isn't long and wild anymore; she now cuts it into a short trendy hairdo, and has become more domesticated then she would like to admit.

I, on the other hand, still looked the same, with my messy golden brown hair swept over to the side. And, unlike Elli, I tend to be withdrawn, enjoying the little things, such as reading anything and everything, learning new languages, and traveling. But most of all, I love my time with Maiko.

Recently I had been giving lectures at a University of Illinois at Chicago (UIC) on the History of the Supernatural. I had become an expert in all things Supernatural, or at least the things about the supernatural world that I was allowed to share. My lectures are mostly about my life and my own experiences. To date, I have now written twenty-five fantasy and mystery books in several different series, and six books on historical time periods, one being an historical autobiography.

This particular evening, I was giving a late lecture on the Roaring Twenties and how vampires played a role in it. Elli loved the Roaring Twenties. She loved the jazz clubs, drinking whiskey (though it was not the same as blood), and gambling with high-profile mobsters whose names I prefer not to mention. Vampires, being privy as we were to all the goings-on of the seedy late-night underworld, played a huge role in Prohibition, the backroom clubs frequented by brassy flappers, the Mob, and, of course, the gambling, and now that we were out, the human world was eager to learn about our secret history.

As I started back up the stairs towards my room, Maiko was instantly next to me, loyal to the end. I packed up my books and my laptop, trying to fit as much as I could into my messenger bag. Then Maiko and I made our way back down the stairs.

"We're leaving. See you soon."

"You're taking Maiko? They let dogs in lecture halls?"

Maiko and I both turned and looked at Elli. I shook my head. "Maybe not ordinary dogs, but vampire dogs . . . absolutely." I smiled. Maiko make a harrumphing sound, wiggled her tail, then followed me out of the house.

We walked out of our front door into the night. I had parked my new 2012 BMW X6 M in front of our house on Oakley Avenue nestled in the Bucktown neighborhood. Shawn, Elli and I had purchased several properties all over the U.S., Canada, and the Virgin Islands, but of all our places, this cozy four-bedroom house was most like home. Though we would be gone for periods of time, sometimes together, sometimes separately, we always came back to this place, our home. Usually, I parked my car in the garage, but I had had to run some errands earlier that day for Shawn.

I opened the passenger door and Maiko jumped in. I moved around to the driver's side and took off up Oakley Avenue, taking a left onto Fullerton and then merging on to the Kennedy Expressway heading towards UIC.

When I arrived at UIC, I parked in the Professors' section of the North Parking lot. I got out and walked across Harrison Street and into the Behavioral Science Building and past the big lecture hall on the second floor. I went to Professor Jordan's temporary office and knocked, but he didn't answer. I went back towards the lecture hall and the doors were still shut. The entranceways were starting to get crowded. Maiko became agitated being in close quarters with so many humans.

I whispered, "Settle down, Maiko. Be a good girl."

"Do you always bring your dog wherever you go?" I looked up to see a girl in her early twenties, with blond hair, beautiful blue eyes, and a huge grin across her face.

I smiled back. "Yup. I take her everywhere."

"So she likes lectures and vampires? But crowds not so much, I see."

"You're right about that. She definitely doesn't like crowds." We started to move in with the crowd that was pushing into the lecture hall as we carried on our conversation. "Are you a student at UIC?"

"I am," she replied. I noticed she was moving a huge

silver ring around her ring finger on her right hand. "Have you been to one of Evin Driscol's lectures before? This is my first time. I only recently read his historical work *Vampires and Their Impact on the Roaring Twenties*. It was quite interesting, and a little terrifying." I turned to look at her as she sat down in the middle aisle seat in the third row and I grinned.

Then I continued up to the front of the lecture hall. I recognized Professor Jordan at the podium asking everyone to please sit down. We shook hands, and he raised his eyebrow at me.

"Hello, Evin. Glad you could make it."

"I wouldn't have missed it," I retorted. He hated my habit of showing up at the last minute.

Professor Jordan turned to the audience and announced, "Please welcome Dr. Evin Driscol, author of twenty-five fantasy and mystery novels, five historical studies on vampire life and one historical autobiography. He is here to give a brief description of his life and speak about how vampires played a significant role in the Roaring Twenties."

I stepped up to the mic and patted Maiko on the head next to me. My incisors came out for everyone to see. I looked towards the young woman in the third row, who appeared to be blushing, and smiled. I then looked up to the packed 250-person lecture hall and began. "Hello. My name is Dr. Evin Driscol and I am a vampire; but among vampires, I am known as a Daywalker."

THE CHOSEN HISTORIAN

Chapter 4

AFTER the lecture, I did my routine of answering a few questions and giving autographs. I noticed that several people were asking me to sign my new book, *Vampires and Their Impact on the Roaring Twenties*, which pleased me greatly. I noticed that the girl I had spoken with prior to the lecture was still sitting in the same seat as before. As I made my way through the crowd towards her, Elli walked up with her friend. Great.

"Evin, great lecture! You should have told them about that night the bar got raided on Thirty-fifth Street."

"Some things don't need to be shared, Elli," I

commented. "And you are—?" I asked, looking over to the blond girl standing next to Elli.

"My name is Jasmine."

"Sorry, Jasmine, this is my brother Evin. Evin, this is Jasmine."

"So I'm told," I responded, somewhat snooty. "It's nice to meet you, Jasmine. Elli tells me you're in her art class?"

"I am. This is actually our second class together."

"Ah. Elli didn't mention that," I said absentmindedly. I looked over to see if the blond girl from before the lecture was still there. She was. "Elli, do you mind taking Maiko home with you? I have something I need to do."

Elli gave me an inquisitive look. "Sure, Evin." Maiko looked miffed.

"Be a good girl, Maiko, and go home with Elli. I'll see you when I get home." I turned to Jasmine. "It was nice meeting you. I'm sure I'll see you again." With that, I made my way towards the blond-haired girl with the blue eyes and sat down next to her. "You're still here."

"I am. You know, you could've told me who you were." She tried to sound angry, but I could sense she was more embarrassed than anything else.

"I could have. Or you could have just asked me who I was." I directed a smile towards her and she smiled back. "Would you like to go get a drink with me?" She looked a little thrown off by this.

"Sure, but only if you're going to be honest with me," she replied curtly.

"I was never dishonest. How about this: I promise to tell you what you want to know, but only if you ask the right questions. If I were to just offer information, it would take a human lifetime to hear it."

She smiled then said, "Before we start talking about a lifetime, let's start with a nice getting-to-know-you conversation over drinks. My name is Kathryn Riley, but everyone calls me Katie."

"It's nice to meet you, Katie Riley." I smiled. "My name is Evin Driscol."

****

I opened the door to Holy Ground, a local bar for

vampires. Katie stopped in front of the door and appeared hesitant to go in. It was clearly the first time Katie had been to a supernatural joint.

"Have you never been to a supernatural bar before?" I inquired. "This is known to be a hot spot for the local vampires. I like to come here every now and again, but if you want to go somewhere else, we can."

Katie turned to me and gave me a faint smile. "You're right, I haven't been to a vampire bar before. But I'm willing to try anything once."

"Good. You don't have to worry about anything. You're safe with me." Katie smiled and stepped through the door, with me following her.

We walked over to the far side of the bar to one of the available tables. As we made our way across the room, I noticed the majority of the vampires in the bar were looking our way, particularly at Katie. Katie was a beautiful girl, nothing like most fang-bangers, who usually looked like Goth chicks, whores, or crackheads. Katie looked like a college girl raised in that perfect nuclear familiar, though I sensed she had a wild side, too. I could also sense that Katie noticed the stares as well, but she continued to appear confident.

As we sat down, Katie asked, "Why is everyone staring at us?"

"They're not staring at us. They're staring at you."

"Okay, why are they staring at me, then?"

"Because you don't look like a fang-banger."

She cracked a smile. "That's because I'm not a fang-banger," she chuckled.

"That's good to know. I was worried you were just trying to hook up with me," I said sarcastically with a smile.

She smiled back. "Well, I'm glad we set the record straight."

We both grew silent for a moment, not knowing what to say next. Why was I here with her? It was unlike me to invite a total stranger out for drinks, especially after a lecture. I hated groupies and fang-bangers. But I knew she was neither.

One of the vampire waitresses walked up during our awkward moment to take our orders. "What are you having?" she asked.

I looked to Katie and nodded for her to order first. "I'll have a Jameson on the rocks," she said.

I smiled. This was my type of girl, one who could hold her Irish whiskey.

"What are you having, honey?" the waitress asked me.

I continued looking at Katie as I responded, "I will have a Bloody Paddy."

The waitress made a disgusting grunt and whisked away.

"What's up with her?" Katie asked.

"I believe she has an issue with you being a beautiful human woman. But don't worry, she probably dislikes all human women, whether they're beautiful or not."

Katie started to blush. "What's a Bloody Paddy?"

"It's actually called Bloody Paddy Synthetic Whiskey. It's supposed to be smooth like Irish whiskey. It was developed by an Irish fellow who is now a vampire."

"Wow, so you don't have to drink blood at all?"

"No, we don't have to drink blood, though some still prefer it. My sister Elli and I have never really had to drink blood like the others." Why did I feel the need to explain myself to this girl?

"So you don't like to drink blood?"

"I do like blood. I like it a lot. But the topic is—complicated."

"Oh." Katie looked at me curiously, but I could tell she knew I was not going to say anything more about this topic.

"So you mentioned before the lecture that you read my book *Vampires and Their Impact on the Roaring Twenties.*" I was trying to change the subject and figure out why she was here with me.

"I'm taking History 425, the Roaring Twenties, and one of the books we're reading in that class is your book." I noticed she was blushing, though she kept eye contact extremely well—for a human.

"So you must be taking Professor Jordan's class, then," I replied.

"Yes. I really like Professor Jordan. His teaching methods are quite unusual, which I really find refreshing. He mentioned in class that he knew you?"

I smiled, fascinated by her interest in the details of my

life that had nothing to do with me being a vampire. "Well, I have known Jakob—excuse me, Professor Jordan—since he was a young boy. He used to run errands for me to make money to help his family and save for college."

"Wow, he has to be in his late fifties," she said, shocked that Jakob could have ever been a young boy to me; even though she knew better, I still looked like I was in my mid-twenties.

"Actually, he's seventy-four. I met him when he was nine years old and his father had just passed away. It was the Forties. His mother was really young, and he was the oldest of five children. He was begging for work on the block where I lived. He actually lived just a few blocks from me." I could tell Katie was fascinated by my story.

The waitress walked up with our drinks. She set my Bloody Paddy in front of me, and slammed Katie's Jameson down on the table a little harder than I thought was necessary.

"Thanks." The waitress walked away without answering. "As I was saying, he was trying to find work. I had been watching him for days out my den window begging for odd jobs from strangers on the street. One day, I walked out to him and asked him what kind of work he could do. He said, 'Anything that wouldn't upset my mother.' I couldn't help laughing at that, even though I could tell it made him mad. I asked him why he wanted to work when he should be focusing on his schoolwork, and he told me it was because his family needed him and he wanted to go to college. I knew then that this kid had potential to be a great man. So I paid him a hundred and fifty dollars a week, with a ten-dollar-a-week increase each year until he was nineteen. He ended up paying off is mother's mortgage, with a little help." I smiled a little because I remembered paying off the balance on the overpriced home. "And he ended up having enough money for college."

"Wow. You must really like Professor Jordan."

"I do like Jakob. When I met him he reminded me of myself when I was young."

We both grew silent for a few moments, looking down into our drinks, unsure of what to say next. I slowly looked up, just as she did the same, and our eyes meet. We both looked down quickly. Why did I feel so nervous? What was it about this girl? I looked up at her again. She was beautiful, with her honey-blond hair and clear blue eyes, but there was more to it than that. I sensed something different about her, something familiar and yet completely unique at the same time, different than most human girls. I also noticed she was playing with her ring again.

"Was your ring a gift?" I inquired.

She looked down at it, unaware she'd been fiddling with it. "Thanks. It's been in my family for generations. It was my seventh great grandmother's. It has been passed through each generation to the first born girl. My mother wore it when I was a kid, and then she gave it to me when I went away to college."

"It's beautiful," I commented.

"Thank you." She paused thoughtfully, then changed the subject. "So, how old are you, if you don't mind me asking? Of course, if you don't want to say, I can just pick up your autobiography tomorrow," she commented playfully.

"I was born in 1841. I am one hundred and seventy-one

years old."

"You look good for an old man," she said with a giggle. I laughed too.

"Thanks. I age well," I took a sip of my drink. "And how old are you, if you don't mind me asking?"

"I just turned twenty-two."

"What year are you in school?"

"My fourth year, thank goodness. I am *so* ready to be done with school. I plan to take a year off before going to grad school."

I found myself so focused on her that I could hear her pulse beating faster and faster as we continued our conversation. Did that mean she liked me? Did I like her?

"It's starting to get late, and I really should get back home before my roommates start to worry about me."

"Sure. I'll take you home." I threw plenty of money on the table to cover the tab and we both got up to leave.

We sat quietly in the car as I drove her home. She lived in the Little Italy neighborhood near UIC. I pulled up to her apartment building, a classic three-level stone building built in the early twentieth century. "Thank you for the drink." She turned to face me in the car.

"You're welcome." I found myself smiling. "Let me get your door for you."

I got out of the car and was around to the other side in the blink of an eye. I could tell that my supernatural vampire speed shocked and impressed her. I opened the door and put out my hand for her to hold on to as she got out of the car. She continued to hold my hand as I walked her up the front steps to the door, then she turned to me and smiled.

"Thanks, Evin, for taking me to my first vampire bar."

"And I'm glad that your first time was with me. I mean..." I could feel the blood rising in my face. "—your first trip to a vampire bar." I paused to gain my composure. "Maybe we can see each other again," I said, rather hopefully. I continued to hold her hand, and then reached out and grabbed her other hand. I noticed we were nervously swinging our hands a little together, as if we weren't sure what to do with them.

"I'd like that."

Katie looked me in the eyes. I leaned in to kiss her

and found my lips meeting hers. Hers were warm and soft, unlike mine, which are always cold. She reached up around my neck, pulling herself closer to me, and I caught the sweet scent of her skin. Our kiss seemed to last a long time—but not long enough. As she pulled away from me her face was flushed.

"Good night, Evin." She turned, opened the door and went in. Before she shut the door behind her, she turned around and smiled at me. Of course, I smiled right back, fangs and all.

THE CHOSEN HISTORIAN

⌒ↄ Chapter 5 ↄ⌒

AS I lay in bed that night, I found myself thinking of Katie. I imagined her smile, her blue eyes, and her soft lips. I wanted to see her again, to smell her again, and to brush my face against her soft hair. I would make sure to see Katie again soon. Really soon.

Maiko jumped onto the bed and nudged me with her nose. I pulled her close to me and hugged her. "I love you too, Maiko." And then we feel asleep together.

When I woke, Maiko was not next to me. I rolled up out of bed, went over to my stereo, and turned on some U2. God, I love U2. I remember when the band first called themselves Feedback and The Hype. I used to go see their shows in London with Shawn and Elli. As *Sunday Bloody Sunday* started to play, I took a shower, letting the warm water flow over me. I loved hot showers as much as I loved U2.

When I got out of the shower, I quickly dressed and sat down at my laptop. I decided to Google Katie, although I'm not sure why I felt the need. I found out she played rugby for UIC and that she'd been a soccer player in high school. She had been offered several soccer scholarships all over the U.S., but she had turned them down to go to UIC. I thought that was odd. Why would she turn down a full scholarship to the University of North Carolina to go to UIC? I also found out that she was from Fayetteville, North Carolina, and that her mother was a famous biochemist.

I got up from my desk and sat down on my bed, reaching underneath to grab my favorite pair of Devz shoes. I love my Devz shoes, mostly because I own stock in the company, but also because for every pair of shoes they sell they give three pairs to a people in need in a Third World country. I had spent enough decades traveling the globe to know what extreme poverty looked like.

I looked at myself in the mirror. I was wearing one of my many v-neck t-shirts, white, with my favorite pair of jeans, and my slip-on Devz. My golden hair was in its usual style, messy and hanging around my face. Elli always says that Zac Carey from *Vampire Within* must have met me at some point and stolen my hair style. Ridiculous, but I had to admit, his hair style *was* exactly like mine, color and all.

I made my way downstairs and into the kitchen, grabbing a synthetic drink out of the refrigerator and knocking it back. Then I went into the living room and found Maiko snuggled up with Elli on the couch watching *Vampire Within*. Elli loves that show, because it's one of the first vampire shows to ever depict our lives with any kind of accuracy. I have to admit I secretly like it as well, but I try not to let Elli know, or think about it when I'm around her.

"Where are you going this evening?"

"I think I'm going to go for a bike ride, then go over to visit Jakob." Maiko got off the couch and came over to me, ready to go. "You have to stay here, girl. I'm going on a bike ride tonight." Maiko gave me a disappointed look and jumped back into Elli's lap.

"I think you hurt her feelings, Evin."

"Maiko will be okay. Just make sure to feed her."

"Of course," Elli said sarcastically. "Where were you last night, by the way?"

"I went to Holy Ground last night with a girl I met."

"A human girl?"

"Yes, a human girl." I did not want to talk about this with Elli right now and said so in my thoughts, so she didn't ask me about it again.

I went out the back door to our three-car garage. Tucked in next to my BMW was my custom motorcycle. I got on and took off down the alley and out onto Lyndale Avenue. Instead of going straight to Jakob's, I rode around Bucktown thinking about Katie, and I soon found myself driving south towards her house. When I got there, I sat out in front for about twenty minutes trying to decide if I was going to go and knock.

"Evin? What are you doing here?" I turned around to see Katie looking at me with her arms full of textbooks.

How did I let myself get caught off guard?

"Umm, hi. I was . . . cruising around Bucktown and . . ."
I felt nervous.

"But this is Little Italy," she commented curiously.

"Yeah, I sorta ended up here. Not that here is a bad
place or anything." Oh God. I sounded really stupid. "Um, I
was wondering, if you weren't busy, maybe you would want
to hang out for a while?"

Katie smiled. "Sure. Let me take my books inside."

"Here, let me carry them for you." I moved off my bike
and she handed me her books. I followed her up the stairs
to her front door. She unlocked it and went in, not noticing
I had hung back, staying outside on the porch. I had to—I
couldn't go in, because I hadn't been invited. Of course, she
had no idea that was one myth about vampires that was
actually true. We can enter public buildings no problem,
and places occupied by other vampires, but if we try to
enter a human residence uninvited, it's like bumping into
an invisible wall. It can really be embarrassing.

She turned around and gave me a curious look. "Come
in. I don't bite," she said, and with a sarcastic smile she

turned and started walking down the hallway. I stepped over the threshold and followed her.

To the right was the living room followed by the dining room, obviously used as a study because of all the books spread out covering the dining room table. Next to the dining room was the kitchen. On the left side of the hallway were two bedrooms with a bathroom in between. Towards the back was a stairwell that Katie began to walk up, and I followed her. At the top of the stairs were two doors, one door to a tiny bathroom, and the other leading to her bedroom. When she opened the door, I was amazed at how beautiful it was for such a small space. The walls were slanted in, leaving little headroom by the south and north walls. Her desk faced out the window on the west wall. Her bed was very low to the floor, and she had huge fall-colored cushion pillows all over the room. The walls were blended burnt oranges, browns, yellows, and reds. She had homemade tapestries in fall colors hanging down in the corners as well. I set her books down on her desk.

"I like your room. Did you do this?" I spun around slowly, taking everything in. "I mean, did you paint and design this room yourself?"

Katie started to blush. "My mother helped me. She's a lot more talented than I am, but I did pick out the colors. I just couldn't stand the sterile-looking white walls."

She sat down on her bed and patted the spot next to her. I laughed at the thought that she was commanding me to come to her. I moved over to her a little faster than the average person—not as fast as I could have, of course, but I could tell my quickness surprised her.

"You look beautiful." Our faces were inches apart.

"You look pretty good yourself," she responded.

"You're not afraid of me? Afraid I will hurt you?"

She smiled. "If you were going to hurt me, I would think you would have done it by now. Plus, I have never heard or read anything about you taking a human life. In fact, Professor Jordan says you don't need much blood to sustain yourself, and that you prefer synthetic blood."

"Well you're right about one thing. You'll never read about me taking human life because I don't write about it. But I have taken a life before. I'm not proud of it, and it's not something I like to talk about." I looked down, ashamed.

"Evin," she grabbed my chin and forced me to look up at her. "I know you would never hurt anyone, especially me," then she leaned in and kissed me. Her soft lips warmed my own. The next thing I knew, we were enveloped in each other's arms. "Evin, I'm so glad you're here."

I kissed Katie on her forehead. "I'm glad I'm here too. I feel like I could just lie here with you all day and forget the rest of the world." She smiled at that, and we continued snuggling.

"I've never felt like this about anyone, Evin. I'm really drawn to you." Katie moved her body over mine and started kissing my neck while she pressed against me. I moaned and she responded by moving her body against mine. I pulled her head towards mine and kissed her feverishly all over her face and her lips. I rolled her over so I was on top and pressed myself against her. Our tongues intertwined while our bodies continued to move against each other.

"I am not hurting you, am I?" I asked between kisses.

Katie moaned and responded to my question by pulling me tighter to her. We were both engulfed in the moment. Time seemed to stand still. Then suddenly, Katie rolled back on top of me and sat up, her hair disheveled and even sexier than usual.

"Evin, I have to tell you something. Last night after you left, I saw a man standing outside my apartment. He was across the street looking directly at me through my window. It was really creepy."

"Was it right after I left?"

"Yes. I was watching you get in your car and leave when I noticed him across the street. He was actually watching you, then he looked up at me."

"I never noticed or sensed anyone around when I left." This was odd. As a vampire, I could always sense a presence in my vicinity. If he was human, I should have heard his heartbeat and breathing; if it was another vampire, I would have been able to sense him telepathically. "What did he look like?"

"He had dark hair that hung to his shoulders and intense eyes. He was dressed really nice, in a sweater and dark jeans. That was all I could see. But you know what was funny—as soon our eyes met, he smiled, and then he was gone. I almost feel like I imagined him."

I grew silent thinking about this for a minute. So, he had been watching me, had made sure Katie saw him, and then had vanished instantaneously. Sounds like a vampire. The thing about vampires is that we have a lot of different gifts, some of which are common to all of us—speed, superior senses, the ability to heal quickly and to put humans in a trance. However, some vampires, a very small group of us, develop unique gifts, many of which are not public, because the Federation does not want the human race to know (the backlash and red tape we would have to go through to register these traits would be terribly inconvenient). My gift, which I shared with my sister, was that we could read each other's thoughts as long as we were within a few miles of each other, and, of course, that we could walk in the sun. If I concentrated, I could also move things with my mind; Elli could climb walls and disappear for short spurts of time.

Katie kissed me on the lips. "Evin, where are you? I was

telling you about that man, and then you kind of zoned out on me."

I returned her kiss and then rolled her off to the side of me so I could get up. "I'm sorry. I was just thinking about what you were saying."

"Are you leaving? It seems like you just got here." Katie stood up and moved towards me.

"I think I should go. I have to work on a few things at home, and I also need to visit with Jakob. I'll call you later tonight." I cupped her face in my hands and softly kissed her lips. "Promise."

"Okay, but I better see you soon," she replied and smiled.

Katie walked me to the door, and I turned to meet her eyes. "If you see this man again, tell me right away. Do not confront him. Also, do not invite any strangers in."

"Why would I invite a stranger in?" she asked, insulted at my suggestion that she'd do something so dumb.

"It's just . . . if he is a vampire, he can't come in if you don't invite him."

"So that myth at least turns out to be true."

I smiled. "It is. And sometimes it can be a good thing. I'll see you later." With that, I turned and left.

～⟲ Chapter 6 ⟳～

"JAKOB, who do you think it is? I wonder what he wants from Katie or me?" I flopped down on Jakob's old worn leather couch in his den. Jakob's home was always a huge mess, with books, research notes, and student papers scattered all over.

"I don't know, Evin, but you must find out. And be careful doing it." Jakob sat at his desk concentrating on his laptop. I was sure he was searching the Federation database of registered vampires.

"I'm trying to think of a vampire we know that fits his description. Katie said that he was gone suddenly. She didn't use the word 'vanished,' which tells me he could have moved so quickly she just didn't see him leave. But he could have actually vanished. Do we know any vampires that vanish?"

Jakob kind of keeps track of my life history, like a guardian, in a way. It's kind of funny if you think about it. I'm the one who saved him, but he's the one who ends up looking out for me all the time. He has even been given special approval to access the Federation database, because he's one of only a few humans to be known as an expert in vampire history and culture.

He appeared deep in thought for a few moments, then said suddenly, "You do know someone who can vanish, Evin. Sebastian. I remember when I was a young boy, you told me about what it was like when you all lived together as a coven. You told me Sebastian could just materialize in the room, which always freaked you out." He continued to stare at the laptop while talking to me.

I jumped up in excitement. "You're right, Sebastian *could* vanish! How could I forget? He does somewhat fit her description, too."

"I looked him up here in the database. It has a picture of him. His last whereabouts are listed as New York in the 1950s. No one has seen him since. It's like he just disappeared. Take a look at his file, Evin."

I moved over to Jakob and looked over his shoulder at the screen. There was an old picture of Sebastian wearing a fedora and pinstriped suit. His hair was dark, about shoulder length with a little wave to it. Debonair and perfect, as always.

"It says here that he used to live with another vampire, Niklas Urz, until the 1920s, and that he lived and traveled by himself after that, at least until he disappeared."

"Does it say where Niklas is now, or why Sebastian left?"

"No, it doesn't say anything about why he left. It does say that Niklas has had some trouble with the Federation, and has been punished for several crimes. It looks like he's lived in several locations—New York, Boston, San Francisco, Munich, Rome, and Paris. It doesn't say what his current status or location is, though."

"What was he charged for? He was always a bad apple."

I disliked Niklas, and Jakob knew why.

"For turning several humans and letting them run rampant. He was also charged with torturing a human. It says his punishment was to be buried for one year in the House of Gods, where he was fed once a month through a hose."

Oh shit. It would make any vampire go crazy to be buried for so long, though I've heard of the elders burying some vampires for a lot longer. It would also make a lot of vampires crazy to go that long without blood, or at least synthetic blood. I knew Niklas had to be pissed.

"They don't know where he is now?"

"It says 'location unknown.' Let's just hope he's not around here."

"In the meantime, we need to find this man, whether he is Sebastian or not. I don't like the idea of someone following me or knowing about Katie. If something happens to her . . ."

Jakob looked at me and began to smirk. "You like this girl?" he asked—but it sounded more like a comment than a question.

"She's not like any other girl I have ever met. Yes, I like her a lot."

****

I walked into the kitchen and went straight to the refrigerator for a drink. I downed a cold Animus, one of the many bottled animal blood options on the market, savoring the taste. It was good, but I like Bloody Paddy better, the reason being that it tends to have a warmer flavor, and warmer blood always tastes better. Lost in the savoring of the taste, I heard Elli speak to me through our thoughts. I could sense she was in the living room, off the kitchen.

Evin, we have company.

I turned to see Elli standing by the fireplace, Shawn seated in the recliner, and the man Katie had described sitting on the couch.

"Hello, Sebastian," I said, moving into the living room with lightning speed and sitting down in the chair across from the couch.

"Hello, Evin. I am sure you are wondering why I am

here," Sebastian said in a calm voice.

"I am curious. I'm also curious as to why you are following me and standing outside my girlfriend's house." Elli and Shawn both turned their heads towards me with surprised looks on their faces.

"So she told you she saw me, I take it."

"She did. So what is it that we can help you with, Sebastian?"

"I did not come here to fight with you or cause you any problems. I am sorry that it seems as though I have been following you. I have been hiding in the shadows for so long that my social skills have grown somewhat lacking. I have come here to discuss a few things with all of you. I followed you because I wanted to make sure you weren't being followed by someone else. Someone other than me."

"Who would be following us, Sebastian? Where's Niklas?" Elli demanded.

"Well . . ." he paused as if he needed to contemplate how to say what he was about to say next. "I am not sure where Niklas is, though I believe that he is coming here to find all of you. I was following you Evin to make sure that he was not already here."

"So you're not with Niklas anymore," Shawn remarked, unsurprised. "Why would you think he would be looking for us? What would Niklas want with us?" Shawn and Elli shared a glance.

"First I must tell you what happened between us." Sebastian paused and crossed one leg over the other. "Niklas and I did fairly well for ourselves after the three of you left. Our income grew, along with our property. However, Niklas became obsessed with his hunting. You remember how he enjoyed the kill, and how he had begun to torment his victims. Well, he ended up getting into trouble with both human law and the Federation. Women were disappearing during the Chicago's World Fair, and law enforcement thought they were dealing with some new type of serial killer. What they did not realize was that it was Niklas."

Everyone was silent and focused intently on Sebastian and his story. We all knew that Niklas was evil, and that what he had been when we knew him was only the beginning.

"Niklas and I begun to argue and fight. I grew tired of his games and his ways. I told him that I would no longer stand by and watch him behave so abominably. I told him the humans would eventually figure out who or what he was, and I did not want the wrath of the elders upon us."

"That was all you were concerned with? Getting in trouble with the elders?" I responded with disgust.

"No, that was not all. I did not like what he was becoming. You know I never enjoyed torturing and playing with my victims. But as you well know, Niklas could always charm me. I would disapprove again, and again, but the next thing I knew, I was giving in to his indulgences. I know . . . it was wrong, and I let it go on for too long." I could sense sadness in Sebastian's voice. He pulled out an old pocket watch from somewhere in his jacket and began to open and close it absentmindedly as he continued.

"Niklas stopped torturing his victims for awhile. Law enforcement did end up catching a serial killer during the World's Fair and charged him with all the murders, though most of the victims were really Niklas's. I thought he was finally finished with his silly behavior, but I was wrong. In the late 1910s, Niklas began to enjoy the night life. By the time the Roaring Twenties came, Niklas was carousing every night in the mobster bars, spending more and more of his time with whores, and even turned a young man to share in his escapades. At first it was one, but then he began to turn more."

"How many did he turn? Why didn't you stop him?" I asked.

Sebastian snapped the pocket watch shut. "He turned four young men. I tried to convince him that it was too many, that he would never be able to control them or teach them, but he would not listen." Sebastian paused. "I couldn't kill Niklas. I just couldn't do it. I loved him even if he had changed, and I was unable to control him. I did kill two of his fledglings, the worst two. This was difficult, because as you know, I have the right to kill my own fledglings, but not those of others. However, the elder council let me go unpunished. By the time I finally finished them off, they had become absolutely out of control, the worst of the worst, wreaking havoc and killing anybody they came across, vampire or human. Niklas was angry with me for killing his fledglings, and even struck me. After that, I left him, in 1923. I essentially vanished. I continued to follow Niklas because I felt responsible for him, but he never knew. I lost him in New York in the 70s and haven't been able to find him since. I sometimes hear stories and follow the leads, but I have never seen him myself."

Everyone was quiet. Sebastian tucked the watch back into his jacket pocket.

Shawn spoke up. "I had heard of Niklas's, er, issues, when we came back to Chicago in the 1920s, but thankfully, we never saw him. Why do you think he's here? And why would he be looking for us?" Shawn asked.

"I followed his trail to Burlington, Iowa in the 50s. He went there to find your descendants."

Elli looked mortified. She and I had thought about looking in on our siblings and their children, but we never did.

"What did he do, Sebastian? Did he harm our family?" I could sense that my emotions were starting to show because my voice had started to rise.

"No, he did not harm them. But he did not get what he wanted from them, either."

"What could he possibly want from our family?" I demanded.

"He wanted to find out why you and Elli are different. Why you can walk in the sun."

"How could he possibly find that out from them? They didn't know anything about it, about us! *We* don't even know why we have this gift!" cried Elli, distraught.

"By drinking their blood," Shawn answered. "He must have discovered that drinking their blood didn't change him, so they couldn't be the key." He looked to Sebastian. "Why didn't he kill them?"

"Because he did not know if Elli and Evin were watching over them. He did not want to take the chance that you would come after him. He put them in a trance and made them forget he had feed from them, or that they had even seen him."

"Okay . . . so, where did he go after that?" asked Elli, struggling to maintain her composure.

"I followed him to Dublin, Ireland right after. He

was searching for someone there. I believe it was your sister Noami. But I believe he did not find her."

"That's near where our family is from. Are you sure he didn't find her?" I questioned.

"I don't know. I am not positive. What I do know is that your younger sister Noami moved from Burlington when she turned eighteen and traveled the world, eventually moving to Dublin. But I could not find her there. She would have been quite old by that time, so it's possible she could have passed away some time before. I could not find any of her direct descendants, so I believe she had no children."

"You mean Noami just vanished? Do you think he could have found her and harmed her, do you?" Elli said, alarmed again.

"I don't know," said Sebastian. "But I don't think so. I really do not think he found what he was looking for. Which leads us here. I think he has searched in vain for answers for a long time, and now he's going to come here. For you."

Everyone grew quiet again.

↶ Chapter 7 ↷

SEBASTIAN didn't stay. He told us he would be in touch and let us know if he saw or heard anything about Niklas arriving in Chicago. We all sat around in the living room reflecting on the information he had shared with us.

Shawn broke the silence, turning first to look at me. "So you have a girlfriend now?" He took a sip of his coffee.

"Well, she's not my official girlfriend, but Katie is definitely important to me." I tried unsuccessfully not to blush.

"And when did this take place? Why haven't we met her? Who is she?" Elli blurted out the questions. It was obvious she was still upset by Sebastian's visit.

"A girl I met at my lecture. The one I was out with last night." I shifted uneasily in my chair. I didn't much like personal questions, and even when it was my own sister grilling me.

"Well, you should bring her by, Evin, though I would wait until this whole Niklas thing is over with. We wouldn't want her to get hurt or worse," Shawn commented.

"I know. I will bring her home eventually, I promise. But I think you're right. I should probably keep away from her for now. If Niklas is here, he might try to hurt her to get to me." I got up and headed towards the stairs.

"Where are you going, Evin?" asked Elli.

"I'm going to call Jakob so he can start investigating Niklas and his two fledglings that we know of. Then I'm going to have to talk to Katie."

***

"Maybe we should talk to the elders and see if they have any more information about Niklas, anything that's not in the database," Jakob suggested.

"I don't know. I hate having to talk to the council. Once they get involved, they start sticking their nose into everything. We don't even know if Niklas is here."

"I would have to agree with Shawn. We need to take this seriously, and Sebastian's hunch is most likely accurate. He knows Niklas better than anybody. And it makes sense that after seeing your family, he would come here to see you, since he desperately wants to discover the key to your gift."

"You're right. My life has been so lax, without complications for so long . . . of course now that I have these feelings for a girl for the first time in ages—a *human* girl, no less—I suddenly have a dangerous vampire looking for me." I flopped back in my chair. "Call me if you hear anything. Maybe you can set an appointment for us to meet with our lieutenant. God, he's such a douchebag. I really hate dealing with him, but I guess we have to go by chain of command. I suppose we can at least meet him, inquire about Niklas, and then voice our concerns and maybe get some protection."

"I think that's a good idea, Evin. Get some rest. Don't forget that tomorrow's Saturday. We have dinner with Kara McCullough. She is interested in discussing your next book deal."

"All right. I'll pick you tomorrow at five. See you then." I hung up my cell phone and lay down on the bed. Maiko jumped up and snuggled in next to me. "Everything is going to be okay, girl," I reassured her, closing my eyes. As I drifted off to sleep, I wondered if I wasn't really reassuring myself.

****

"Katie?"

"Hi, Evin! When am I going to see you again?" Katie asked over her cell.

"How about meeting me for a late dinner at Café Tres in Bucktown?"

"Sure, I can take the Blue Line and be there in forty-five minutes."

"Great. See you then, Katie." We hung up. I walked

down stairs and Maiko followed. "Maiko, do you want some dinner?" She barked, which made me smile, and I patted her on the head. "Sure you do."

She jumped and wiggled her tail excitedly as I poured her some Canine Fury. Then I poured myself some Bloody Paddy Whiskey. Once we finished our snacks I asked Maiko, "Do you want to go on a walk girl?" She answered by jumping up and down excitedly.

It was a beautiful evening with an unusually cool breeze for the time of year. Maiko and I turned onto Lyndale heading towards Café Tres near the Six Corners area of Bucktown.

I love this neighborhood because it's so family-oriented, and everyone is so active and friendly. I like to watch the kids riding their bikes, happy and oblivious to the terrible things that happen outside their safe, clean neighborhood. I like watching mothers pushing strollers and fathers walking their dogs. There's a Senior Citizens Park across the street from my house, and to the left of it is a playground and a swimming pool where most of the neighborhood hangs out during the warmer times of year.

We continued to walk towards Six Corners. Once we arrived at Café Tres, Maiko and I were met by a hostess who sat us in our usual spot on the patio facing the sidewalk. Katie arrived a few minutes later.

"Hi, stranger," Katie said in a flirtatious tone. She leaned down and patted Maiko on the head. "Hi, Maiko. You're so freaking cute!" She scratched Maiko behind the ears, and Maiko responded by leaning into Katie's leg.

"Hey back." I got up and gave Katie a quick kiss on the cheek before we both sat down.

"How has your day been? It's hard to believe it's only been twenty-four hours since we last saw each other. It feels like forever." Katie smiled and leaned over the table, putting her hand on mine. I smiled back and cupped her hand with mine.

"Katie, there's something we have to discuss."

She looked a little worried. "What is it?"

"I can't see you for a while. It's not you . . . or us. It's . . ."

"I don't understand." Her brow furrowed. "I thought you liked me."

"I *do* like you! I like you more than I have liked any girl in a very long time."

"Then what is it? Does it have something to do with that man that was watching you . . . watching us?"

I looked down uncomfortably. "Yes. It does. His name is Sebastian and he's a vampire. He's not a threat, but he believes another vampire might be looking for me. And this vampire who's looking for me is very, very dangerous." I glanced around, sensing something odd in the air.

"Why is this vampire looking for you? Do you know him?"

"I do know him. He used to live with us in a coven after the Civil War. He has always been dangerous, but I'm told he's even worse than ever now. Until I figure out what exactly it is that he wants from me, it's best if you stay away from me for a while. Only when I know things are safe, only then can we continue to see each other." I looked down. I did not want to go a second without seeing her. I wanted to be with her all the time.

"But Evin, I don't want to go without seeing you! I know we haven't known each other long, but it's . . . well, it's almost like we're supposed to be together. I can't explain it. Can't you sense that, too?" She stroked my hand with hers.

"This is only for a little while. I'll call you and check in. You can always call me, especially if you sense something is wrong." I squeezed her hand, looking intently into her eyes.

We both grew quiet, knowing this was for the best right now. We ordered drinks, and the waitress brought them. I tried to relax, but I continued to sense something familiar in the air, but could not figure out what it was. I glanced around, trying not to alert Katie to my uneasiness while we finished our drinks in silence.

"I promise to call you tomorrow night," I said with a hint of sadness that I knew she could sense.

"Okay. But figure this out quick. I want to see you soon . . . to touch you soon," Katie whispered. She grabbed my cheek and kissed me on the lips. She stood up. "I might go home to the suburbs and visit my mom this weekend. I haven't seen her in a while. Please be safe and come back to me soon."

"I will," I promised. She bent down and kissed my

lips again, then turned and walked away. I sat there and watched her dissolve into the crowds of people walking along the sidewalk in the direction of the El train. I looked down at Maiko. "Maiko, let's see what we can do about Niklas," I said, patting her head.

****

Across the street on the patio of the Northside tavern, three vampires sipped Blue Island Bloodies and watched the couple at the table outside Café Tres.

"Niklas . . . is that the vampire that walks in the sun?" asked the young vampire who looked to be about twenty-one, with dark wavy hair and dark eyes.

"Yes, Ralph. I need to know why he can walk in the sun and we can't. Can you imagine what we could get away with if we could move around both day and night? The Federation would never locate us. We would always be a step ahead of them," Niklas said calmly.

"How do you plan to obtain his gift, Niklas?" inquired the third vampire, who was much taller and more muscular than Niklas and Ralph, with piercing blue eyes and brownish-red hair combed into a faux-hawk.

"I am going to taste his blood and drain him dry, Ashton," Niklas replied with a mischievous grin. "Until then, I want you, Ralph, to keep an eye on his sister Elli and her pathetic boyfriend Shawn. Ashton, I want you to follow Evin. It won't be easy. Make no mistake, they are older than you, wiser than you, and can sense when there are other vampires around them, so stay at a distance."

"What do you plan to do while we babysit?" asked Ralph.

"I am going to get acquainted with his lovely friend," Niklas replied, laughing and finishing off his synthetic beer.

∽ Chapter 8 ∾

"THAT will be all for today's lecture on shapeshifters. If you have any questions, please feel free to email me before the exam next week. Remember, this exam is worth twenty percent of your grade, so make sure to review your lecture notes. Good day." Jakob started packing his lecture material into his briefcase.

"Professor Jordan, may I have a word?" Katie had been in the lecture, and was now standing next to him.

"Sure. Katie, isn't it?" He smiled and stopped shuffling his papers. "You have a question about today's lecture?"

"Actually . . . no. I have a question about Evin . . ." she

paused for a moment before finishing her sentence. ". . . and the man who is following him."

"Ah, you assume that Evin has shared some information with me." He knew that Evin had probably told her some things, but he didn't know much about their relationship, or about Sebastian, either.

"I know that you are a good friend and that he trusts you completely. I need to know what's going on."

Jakob could tell it was hard for her to be so open with someone she hardly knew, not to mention her professor. He looked around, then back to her. "Alright, but let's not discuss this in the lecture hall. Why don't you meet me in my office at one this afternoon? I have another lecture before then, but I'm free afterwards."

He needed time to figure out what he should and shouldn't say to her. His next class had an exam, giving him the opportunity to think things through.

"Okay, I'll see you then. Thank you." Katie turned and walked away.

****

"So, Katie, have a sit. What it is that I can tell you that Evin can't?" Jakob sat at his desk, moving papers around as if he were looking for something.

"That's just it. Evin has told me very little. All I know is that a vampire named Sebastian is following him, and that Sebastian warned him that a dangerous vampire is looking for him."

"Well, my dear, Evin has good reason not to share too much info with you. First, there are rules amongst his kind. Secondly, the more you know, the more likely you are to get hurt. And last but not least, if this vampire is dangerous, then it's wise of Evin to put distance between the two of you until this situation is resolved."

"So he does talk to you about everything. I never told you he said we should stop seeing each other until this thing, whatever it is, is over."

"You're right. You didn't say that." Jakob leaned back in his chair. It was obvious to Katie that he was not going to confirm her suspicion that he knew a lot more about the situation than he would admit.

"I'm not asking you to break Evin's confidence. It's just that I'm worried about him. He told me enough to figure out that Sebastian is one of the members of his first coven, and that the other vampire, whoever he is, is another member. I've read some of his autobiography, Professor Jordan. It's not like this is classified information. He used fictitious names, but it's obvious that Sebastian is the vampire he called "Vladimir," and the other vampire that lived in the coven, "Klaus," has to be the one who's looking for him now—whatever his real name is."

"You're right," Jakob admitted. "Evin was given permission to write his autobiography, but there are rules with his kind, and one of those rules is not to expose others to humans. He had to omit certain information, such as the names and gifts or powers of vampires he knew, and other such things as well."

She sat there for a minute contemplating the information that he was sharing, not exactly sure what she was trying to get out of him or what he would actually share.

"Katie, I understand you're worried about Evin, but

he can take care of himself. If you become a target for this dangerous vampire, then you will make Evin vulnerable. Do you understand? Be patient. Evin will sort out this mess, and then you guys can continue to get to know each other."

"I feel so helpless."

"Well, the most important thing you can do to help is to stay away from Evin, and avoid being noticed by this particular vampire."

****

Katie stayed at the library later than usual trying to study for her biology exam, but she gave up when she realized she'd been looking at the same page for the last hour. She couldn't concentrate on cellular respiration. *This is pointless*, she thought. *I can't think about anything but Evin. Might as well call it quits for the night.* With a sigh, she packed up her books to head home.

It was late in the evening. She could hear the low hum of traffic on the highway in the distance, but the campus itself was empty and quiet. Katie continued daydreaming as she walked out of the library and wandered across the plaza towards Morgan Street. *Maybe he didn't really mean what he said,* she thought to herself. *Maybe he'll be waiting on the steps in front of my apartment.* She smiled dreamily as she stepped into Morgan Street, imagining his motorcycle parked on the street in front of her house, when suddenly a car came speeding around the corner, careening towards her. Katie gasped as the blinding flash of headlights froze her in her tracks, unable to move, the screech of the car's tires grating her ears. Before she could scream, she felt herself lifted off the ground—but she hadn't felt any pain. She wondered if this was how it felt to die on impact, but as she slowly opened her eyes, she found herself unscathed on the sidewalk on the other side of the street, in the arms of a beautiful blonde man with greenish-gray eyes.

"Are you okay?" he asked, setting her down gently on the sidewalk.

"I am . . . I guess I wasn't paying attention to where I was going. What happened? It was all so fast!" she gasped, breathless.

"You stepped right in front of that car, but I was able to get you out of the way. You're very lucky, you know."

"Thank you," she managed to say, flustered.

"Don't mention it. I don't get a chance to save a pretty girl every day," he said with a smile that made Katie blush.

"How did you move that quickly? It was as if you flew." As she started to piece together what had happened, she realized no human could move that fast.

"I assure you I did not fly, but I am indeed very fast. But then again, that is not uncommon for a vampire."

Katie tensed. It made perfect sense that the only person who would be around to save her at this late hour would be a vampire, but recent events and her conversation with Jakob made her uneasy. Was this the vampire he had warned her about?

"Are you okay? You look . . . nervous. I assure you that I will not hurt you. After all, why would I hurt you after I just saved you?" He continued to smile.

This sounded logical, and she felt herself slowly begin to relax. "Well, thank you for saving me. I'm sorry if my uneasiness offends you. I don't meet very many vampires."

"I understand." He paused. "We have rules . . . rules that forbid harming humans. Though as I said, I had no plans to harm you. I just saw a beautiful girl who was about to get smashed," he waved his hand in the direction of the street, "by a car."

Katie blushed. She was embarrassed by her reaction to him. She knew that vampires had rules, and she knew that many of them were good-hearted and wouldn't consider harming a human. But she knew that they *could*, all of them, if they wanted to. *My feelings about Evin have given me a kind of sudden familiarity regarding the vampire world*, she thought, *but really, the only vampires I've really even seen besides Evin were the ones in Holy Ground who definitely were not out to make a good impression.*

"Let me carry your books and walk you home. I'd hate for a vampire to jump you in the middle of the night," commented the strange vampire jokingly, as if to put Katie more at ease.

"It's okay, I think I can manage on my own. But thank

you."

"Are you sure? It would be no problem . . ."

Katie cut him off. "No, but thanks."

"Okay, well maybe we will meet again under different circumstances. At least tell me your name?"

"Katie," she paused for a second, wondering if she had made the right choice sharing her name with a strange vampire. "Maybe we will meet again."

"I hope so. My name is Niklas, just in case you want to remember my name the next time we meet." Had she imagined she heard a humorous tone in his voice, as if he knew they would meet again?

"Well, thanks again, Niklas. Have a good night." Katie turned and walked away, heading for home. She felt Niklas watching her until she turned the corner out of sight. On the way home, she felt as if she could sense someone following her, though she turned around several times and saw no one behind her. "Get over it, Katie. No one is following you," she murmured to herself as she quickly headed for home.

****

"I miss you," Katie told me over the phone later that night. We had only known each other a few days, but it felt like we'd known each other all of our lives. Though we hadn't seen each other in almost two days, we continued to talk over the phone and text each other constantly.

"I miss you too. How was your day? How was class?" I lay on my bed looking up at the ceiling, visualizing Katie while she spoke. Ever since the other day at Café Tres, I had thought about her constantly, wondering what she was doing. I hadn't had feelings like this for a girl since Marianne, though I'd been with a lot of women.

"Classes were okay. I spoke to Professor Jordan today." I could sense that she wanted me to inquire about their conversation.

"How is Jakob? I'm having dinner with him and my literary agent tomorrow night." I knew she wouldn't get the answers she wanted from Jakob, so I didn't ask about their conversation, which I knew would surprise her.

"He gave a great lecture today on shapeshifters." She

paused, then asked, "So, you're not going to ask what we talked about?"

"Nope. Jakob will only share what is necessary. He is a smart man and he knows what he can and cannot talk about."

"Huh. Well, I'll have to remember that in the future. He was tough to crack and offered little information." We both grew silent, and the moment became awkward. Katie quickly changed the subject. "I met another vampire today. Well, actually, he saved my life."

My interest was sparked, and I felt suddenly uneasy. If I was really the first vampire she'd ever met, what were the chances she would randomly meet another so soon afterwards?

"I wasn't paying attention to what I was doing when I left the library earlier tonight, and somehow I stepped out in front of a car. Stupid, right? He grabbed me and saved me from being hit. He was nice enough. He had an odd sense of humor, though, which kind of made me feel a little uneasy."

"Well, I'm glad to hear you're all right. What happened

after you almost got hit?"

"He offered to walk me home and carry my books, but I told him that wasn't necessary. Then I left."

"That was it?"

"Well . . ." she had to think about it. "Yes, I guess that *was* it. Pretty anti-climactic. Except he did ask my name, and said that maybe we would meet again someday. Like I said, he was very nice, just a little odd, but kind of cute."

It grated me to hear her say she thought another vampire was cute, but I decided not to comment on it. "Did he offer his name?"

"He said it was Niklas."

****

"Evin, what are you doing?" I paced around her apartment, checking all its hiding places and looking out the windows to see if I could see anyone. Katie followed me from room to room, confused, and waiting for an explanation. "My roommates are going to be home any minute and I don't want you to freak them out, especially since this will be your first time meeting them."

I turned to her and wrapped my arms around her waist. "I'm sorry. It's just that . . . Niklas is the vampire I was telling you about. The one who's looking for me. And now he knows about you, and probably knows where you live, too. He's dangerous and I'm worried about you, but I promise to act like a gentleman when your roommates get home." I pulled her close.

"Wow. Niklas. He's the one who's after you." She paused to take it in, but recomposed herself quickly. "Okay. Well, Sam and Tiff will be home any second. We were planning on ordering a pizza and watching a movie, and of course you can stay. I want you to meet them anyways." She looked up, kissed me on the lips, and whispered, "Maybe you can stay the night, too?"

Of course I wanted that as well. I also knew I needed to figure how to keep her safe now that Niklas knew who she was, and probably knew how much she meant to me. The situation was serious, but it wasn't enough to dampen the effect of Katie's request. She looked up at me expectantly, and I couldn't stop myself from melting. I moved my hand up her back to her hair. She smelled delicious. I pressed my lips to hers, then suddenly scooped her off her feet and tossed her playfully onto the couch. I pretended to lunge at her, leaping lightly onto the couch above her, pulling her into my arms as she giggled. I don't know how we lost track of time, but suddenly it was almost an hour later, and we heard keys jingling in the front door. I jumped up, pulling Katie up into a sitting position with me, trying to make the situation look as innocent as possible. Katie just looked up at me and giggled.

"Well, hello," said one of the two girls walking through the door. "You must be Evin. Cute!" she giggled.

"Don't mind Tiffany. My name's Sam." The other girl put down her books and came over to shake my hand.

"Evin," I responded automatically, though they already knew my name.

"I think we established that," replied Tiffany, warmly and unexpectedly hugging me. "You're cold. Are vampires always cold?"

"Usually colder. I tend to run warmer than most vampires." I smiled, and showed a little fang.

"Is that because you can walk in the sun?" asked Sam, sitting down opposite us in a big armchair while Tiffany perched on the chair's arm rest. Apparently Katie had shared a little information about me.

"I believe so." We all grew quiet.

Tiffany was blond, with dark brown eyes that suggested she probably wasn't a natural blonde, but she was gorgeous all the same. You could tell she was the outgoing and energetic one, the one that had no problem saying what was on her mind. Sam seemed to be more laid back and easy to talk to. She was a sexy brunette with a smile that could light up the room. Together, these three girls were show-stoppers for sure.

I broke the silence. "So, Katie tells me that you're in law school, Tiffany? And that you are in a paralegal program, Sam?"

Tiff responded first. "I'm in my third semester at John Marshall Law School. I've been trying to convince Katie to go to law school, too." She pulled an apple out of her bag and started nibbling. Katie had told me Tiff was a health nut and a fitness junkie.

"Like I've told you a hundred times, I'm not interested in law school." Katie leaned back against the corner of the couch.

"Well, I think you should do whatever makes you happy," Sam responded before turning her attention back to me. "I have a year left at Loyola in the paralegal program."

"Yeah, and when she's done she's going to come work for me," Tiffany commented. Sam smiled and rolled her eyes, and mouthed the word "whatever."

"So how do you all know each other?" I asked.

Katie spoke up. "Well, Tiffany was my big sister in our sorority when we were younger. Sam and I have been roommates since our freshman year when we lived in the dorms. They're like the sisters I never had." They all smiled.

"So, Evin, tell us what you're up to?" Tiffany asked.

"Well, I was just finishing a lecture tour for my book *Vampires and Their Impact on the Roaring Twenties* when I met Katie." Katie grabbed my hand. "I plan to start working on another book that's also about vampire history."

"Neat. Maybe you should have Katie help you! She's really into history. In fact, she has been thinking about applying to a Masters program in History."

I turned to Katie. "Really? You want to be a historian?"

She seemed a little embarrassed. It was clear this was something she wasn't quite ready to tell me. "Um, well, yes. Maybe. I don't know. I think I want to teach Early American History."

"Wow, that's awesome. You never told me this."

"It's no big deal. At least, not until I get accepted."

"Well, maybe I can put a good word in for you at the schools you're applying to."

Sam spoke up. "Tell Evin about how you're trying to trace your lineage."

"Well, like Sam said," Katie started to blush. "I'm trying to trace my family lineage. But I'm sort of stuck right now on my seventh great grandmother. I know where my great grandfather is from, but my great grandmother is another issue. She just sort of appeared. I guess from what my mother says, she was a bit of mystery."

"So are you following your paternal family history, or the maternal side?"

"Definitely the maternal side. The women in my family have always been more interesting and a lot stronger than the men," Katie responded, a little pride in her voice.

"Do you know her maiden name?" I asked. "Maybe I can help you do some research."

"Her name was Marianne Winthrop."

I froze. I couldn't believe it. It took some effort to get my mouth working again. "Marianne Winthrop?"

"Yes, Marianne Winthrop," Katie repeated quizzically.

I really couldn't believe it. Katie was Marianne's seventh great granddaughter. How could this be? My head was spinning.

"Marianne was from Burlington, Iowa," I managed to say.

"How do you know that?" Katie asked, looking confused.

"Because I knew her. We grew up together," I choked out, beginning to feel a little nauseous. I waited for the room to stop spinning. It's times like this that I'm grateful

I don't need oxygen, because I'd go blue in the face before I remembered to start breathing again.

THE CHOSEN HISTORIAN

Chapter 9

"WOW, you knew her?" Tiffany asked excitedly.

"Yes . . . we were schoolmates."

"Wow, that's so awesome! Maybe you can help Katie with her unanswered questions," Sam bubbled. She got up, pulling Tiffany with her. "We'll leave you two alone so you can talk about it some more." Tiffany smiled, then they both headed off to the kitchen.

We were quiet for the next few minutes. It was clear that Katie was not only shocked but unsure of what to ask next.

"How did you know my seventh great grandmother?"

She leaned back from me so she could see my face.

"We grew up together . . . well, sort of. I was poor and her family was wealthy, but that never stopped us from spending time together."

"So you were more than schoolmates, then."

I wasn't sure what I wanted to share with her. It had all been so long ago. That day on State Street in Chicago came flooding back to me, Marianne's eyes locking into mine, only for a second . . . I had relived my moments with Marianne so many times over the years, and I knew I didn't want to relive them again now, especially not here, not with Katie, not like this. But I also knew I needed to tell Katie even if it hurt me.

"We were sweethearts. We were schoolmates as well. We played together and went to school together when we were young, but when we were teenagers, I had to drop out of school to help my family."

"Right. I remember reading that in your autobiography, but you never mentioned her." I could tell Katie was getting frustrated.

"I did mention her, but I gave her a pseudonym. And

I didn't mention her too much, because it was something I didn't quite want to share." I grabbed Katie's hand. "Marianne and I were sweethearts, but her parents didn't like it because my family was so poor. When I went off to war, we lost touch, and when she thought I was dead, her parents quickly married her off to your seventh great grandfather. She moved to Chicago and I never saw her again." I felt terrible for lying, but after all, we hadn't spoken, and I could never be entirely sure that Marianne had seen or even recognized me that day, so what could it matter?

"So let me get this straight. You and Marianne were sweethearts? My seventh great grandmother is your lost love?"

"Yes. She is . . . she was." I didn't know what else to say. Here I had come over to make sure Katie was safe from Niklas only to find out she of all people was Marianne's seventh great granddaughter. I could sense she was feeling as awkward about this as I was. She got up and started to pace around the room, trying to sort everything out in her head.

"Maybe I should go." I stood up to leave.

Katie turned to me suddenly and put both her hands on my chest. "Evin, do you still love her?"

I hesitated, not sure what to say. I couldn't lie, not now. "I will always love her in some way. But she's gone, and I'm still here. I moved on a long time ago. I'm here with you now." I paused for a second and wrap my arms around her. "I am falling for you, Katie. You have completely mesmerized me. I promise you that you are the only one in my thoughts."

Katie leaned up and kissed me softly. "Oh, Evin, that's all I need to know. The fact that you were Marianne's sweetheart—well, it's not easy to wrap my head around. But that was a long time ago." She paused, then looked into my eyes. "Maybe this is just part of the reason why we were meant to meet. As long as you're with me now, I can't be mad at you for loving someone such a long time ago, especially not Marianne." I kissed her again and held her against my chest.

****

"She's Marianne's seventh great granddaughter?" Elli repeated, making sure she had heard me right.

"Yes. She's a descendant of Marianne's." I sat down on the stool in the kitchen with a bottle of Blue Island Bloody.

Elli giggled. "Wow, I can't believe it. I guess you can answer all of her questions about Marianne's youth."

"I guess so. It's not something I really want to discuss, though. At least not right now."

"So does this change anything for either of you?" Shawn inquired. He always tends to be the logical one.

"Not for her."

"So it does for you?" Elli asked pointedly.

"No," I answered reluctantly. "It's just something I'm going to have to get used to. I can't believe the first girl I have liked since Marianne happens to be descended from her. Of all the girls in the world," I took a sip of my beer, shaking my head.

"Sometimes love finds us when we're not looking for it. We have no control over who we fall in love with. We can only control how we respond to it," Shawn commented and yawned, indicating the sun was about to rise.

"Well, I know that I want to be with Katie, so it *is* something I'll have to come to terms with." It occurred to me I was carefully avoiding the word "love." I took another sip of my beer and continued. "After the whole shock thing, I guess we neglected to discuss Niklas. However, Katie assures me her roommates know not to invite anybody in that they don't already know, and they know to be careful around strangers when they're out at night."

"Does that mean she's coming over sooner than later now?" Elli asked with a smile.

"Well," I glanced at my cell phone, noticing it was about six in the morning, "tonight I have dinner with Jakob and Kara, but afterwards maybe Katie could come over and meet the both of you."

"Great! I am *so* looking forward to meeting this girl." Elli turned around and started rinsing out our beer bottles so she could recycle them.

"Well, I'm going to bed. I'll see you tomorrow night, Evin." Shawn wrapped Elli in a passionate embrace and whispered in her ear, "You'll wake me tonight?" I could hear him even though he was whispering, and I knew what he meant.

"Of course, love," Elli whispers back, nibbling his ear.

"Ugh! You know I can hear you." I got up and moved into the living room, settling down on our comfy couch. I heard both of them giggle. A few minutes later, Elli followed me in and snuggled up next to me.

"You know, one of these days you'll find someone you can be like that with," she said reassuringly.

"I think I've already found her," I replied. We sat together in the quiet for a long time, and when I say a long time, I mean a vampire's long time.

"Evin, do you ever wonder what happened to our family?" I could hear the sadness in her voice again.

"Sometimes."

"I always regretted how I left all of you. I miss our sisters and brother. I especially miss Mother."

"They missed you, too. Life happens, Elli. You did what was best for you."

"You never told me what happened to Father and Mother."

"Maybe another time." I didn't want to talk about that now. It was too painful to think about.

"I wonder what happened to Noami. Where did she go? Did she end up meeting some terrible fate?" I could tell this was weighing on Elli.

"Do you really want to know?"

"Yes, Evin. Remember when you said that before you left, mother told you there was something special about the three of us?"

"Yes."

Elli sat up to look at me. "Well, maybe this is the key to why we're different than other vampires. What if what makes us different affected Noami in a different way? Maybe she's still out there."

I thought about this for a second. "How could she still be alive, Elli? The only reason we're still alive—well, still here, anyway—is because we're vampires."

"Think outside the box, Evin. Mother was trying to tell you something important. You know she was a wise woman and only shared when she knew it was important. This thing, whatever it is, that she said was so special about us—maybe it's the key to the way we are. What if it affected Noami a different way? Even if she isn't still alive, and I'm not saying she is, we still need to know what happened to her, Evin."

"I know. We will find out what happened to Noami. I promise." I kissed Elli's forehead.

We had avoided it for so long—for what reason? Guilt? Fear of finding out the truth? Whatever the reason was, I knew the time had come now for us to make sure our family's descendants were all right, and to find out what happened to our sister Noami.

****

"Good evening, Evin," Jakob said, getting into the BMW.

"Good evening, Jakob. Where are we meeting Kara tonight?"

"Joe's downtown."

I love Joe's Seafood, Prime Steak, & Stone Crab. They serve synthetic drinks, but I also enjoy the seafood. Don't get me wrong, I don't need to eat, and sometimes having to digest it can make for an uncomfortable night, but I love food all the same. Sometimes it's worth it to sacrifice your comfort for something you really enjoy.

We pulled up to Joe's and got out. I handed the keys to the valet and we went in.

"Good evening, Dr. Driscol. We have your table ready for you." Did I mention I'm known as a regular here?

"Thank you." We followed him to a table in the back, away from the entrance, in the corner of the room. It's my favorite booth, with little walls to keep out prying eyes; it's where they usually seat famous patrons who want to dine in privacy. "We are waiting on Ms. McCullough. Please escort her back here when she arrives."

"Will do, Sir," the hostess replied and walked away. The server arrived shortly and took our drink orders. I found it a good opportunity to catch up with Jakob.

"So, Jakob, what have you heard?"

"As you know, Lieutenant Van Vechten is still none too happy with you, but he agreed to meet." Jakob tucked his napkin onto his lap and took a sip of water.

"What? Charles is still mad about his girlfriend kissing me? It wasn't even my fault. She kissed me, not the other way around. That was forever ago!"

In fact, that was back in my early vampire years, before leaving Chicago the first time. When I arrived back in town, he'd given me a warning, and I understood it loud and clear. I avoided him at all costs.

"Well, he obviously holds on to grudges. But, like I said, he has agreed to meet. I believe it's only because he feels he has a responsibility to do so. Of course, that doesn't mean that he will actually help you, but I guess we'll find out." He took another sip. "We're meeting him Monday at midnight at his office."

"Well, I promise not to rock the boat with him when we meet. In the meantime, I have to tell you the latest on Katie." I took a sip of my Bloody Paddy Whiskey. "Katie is Marianne's seventh great granddaughter."

Jakob looked up at me from his folder he had just opened on the table, his eyebrow raised.

"Really? How interesting. Who would have thought that the first girl you've dated in decades would turn out to be

Marianne's great granddaughter?"

"Tell me about it." I took another swallow of my Bloody Paddy.

"So how did we figure this out?"

"Well, we were discussing her future as a history teacher. She was telling me about researching her ancestors, and how the trail ended with Marianne. We sort of put it together."

"Katie would make a great history teacher," Jakob commented.

"She would?"

"Oh yes. She retains every fact she learns and tries to take in as much knowledge as she can. She's my best student."

Hearing this made me smile. "Have you ever told her?"

"No. Should I?"

For all his many intellectual talents, sometimes Jakob isn't the brightest when it comes to dealing with other people. "Of course. She seems to be struggling to find herself and what she wants to do with her life. If a professor she admired told her she had a knack for the field, it might help her believe in herself and make a decision."

We looked up to see a tall, dark-haired woman standing suddenly at our table. "Am I interrupting my two favorite men?" She slid into the seat next to Jakob.

"Not at all, Kara. We were just discussing a promising young student in Jakob's class."

"That's good." A waiter came and took our orders. "So how's your new book coming?"

"I haven't really begun, Kara." I knew she wouldn't like this answer.

"Evin, you know your contract says you have to put one out once a year. I wouldn't be such a nag about it, but my boss is constantly on my case."

"I understand. However, since writing some of my historical stuff, I haven't really felt so creative in the fiction department." I took a sip of my drink. "But I promise you I will work on it. I'll have an outline of the book to you in a few weeks."

"Okay. I take it you've been thinking about your next historical book? The world loves your books on vampires and wants more. They also want to know more about the other supernaturals you've talked about in your books."

"I have a few ideas, but remember, this is sort of a tricky subject. You're well aware that supernaturals don't like their business aired out." I took a sip of my drink. "I will keep you updated."

"How's David?" Jakob asked.

"David is good. He's always a little tense just before the full moon." Kara's boyfriend is a werewolf.

"How's the motorcycle business going? I need to take my bike in for a tune-up soon."

"Business is good now. Summer is always his busiest season. Things always slow down for him during the winter."

We continued to chat over our fabulous dinners, discussing possible book ideas and how my lecture had gone. Then we said goodbye to Kara, and I dropped Jakob off at home.

I had been waiting all night to see Katie. I knew she was just as excited to see me, because we'd been texting each other constantly all through dinner. When I pulled up to her apartment, I noticed a car a block or so behind me pull over at the same time. I thought of Niklas and immediately felt uneasy, so when I got out of the car, I didn't go directly to Katie's door. Instead, I walked around to the back of the building and sped behind the other apartments on the block with lightning speed. I was beside the strange car in seconds, grabbing its driver through the open window, who I could now clearly see was a vampire.

"Who are you?" I demanded, baring my teeth.

"I'm Ashton," he responded, his eyes wide, but with a cocky grin playing around the corners of his mouth.

"Okay, Ashton. Why are you following me?"

"Am I following you? I thought I was just parking," Ashton responded sarcastically, though it was obvious he was nervous.

"Don't play with me. I clearly saw you following me. I will only ask you one more time." I tightened my grip on the base of his neck.

"Okay, okay! I *am* following you," he spluttered. I opened the door with my free hand and pulled him out of the car. His eyes widened. "What are you going to do to me?"

"That depends. I don't like to be followed." I pushed Ashton up against his car. "Where is your master?"

"My master?"

He was trying to play dumb, and it irritated me. I pushed harder. "Your master Niklas."

"I don't know where Niklas is, but when I see him next I will be sure to let him know you asked about him." He was trying to sound nonchalant, but I could sense his fear intensifying.

I bared my teeth once more and growled. "Listen to me, errand boy. You tell Niklas that I know why he's here, and that I suggest he forget this absurd fixation of his. Tell him he better get out of town, or it won't be him looking for me anymore. I'll come looking for him, and he'll wish he never came back here."

"Okay, man. Can you let me go now?" I loosened my grip. He straightened up, adjusted his shirt, and got back in his car. I moved onto the sidewalk in case he decided to do something stupid like try to run me over. He didn't, but he glared at me before driving off. I walked back to Katie's place. I knocked on the door and Sam opened it.

"Hey, Evin. Katie's been waiting for you." She stepped aside to let me in.

"Thanks. Upstairs, I take it?" I started in the direction of the stairway.

"Yep." Sam turned around to lock the door. "Are you guys staying in tonight? I have a date so I'm not going to be around, and Tiff is out of town for the weekend."

"I'm not sure. We'll let you know." I smiled and walked towards the back staircase. As I started up the stairs I could hear Kings of Leon playing, and I found myself leaning against Katie's doorway watching her study with all her books spread out on her bed. She looked up at me and smiled.

"I thought I heard someone at the door, but I didn't hear you come up the stairs."

I moved over to kneel down beside her bed and leaned in for a soft kiss. "I'm as silent as a vampire." I smiled and Katie giggled.

"I missed you." She put her arms around my neck. "What do you want to do tonight?"

I thought about it for a second then responded, "Let's see a movie."

"I didn't take you for a movie buff. What do you want to see?"

"I'm not much of a movie buff. Not like Elli, anyway. But I am interested in seeing *Vampire Evolution*." I knew suggesting we see the newest blockbuster vampire flick would crack her up.

She fell back on her bed giggling. "You are the funniest vampire I have ever met." She continued to giggle.

"And how many vampires have you actually met?" I lay down next to her and moved her hair away from her eyes.

"Good point."

****

"What did you think of the movie?" Katie asked as we walked out of the movie into the main lobby.

"I thought it was really good. A little unrealistic, but good. I mean, vampires and werewolves working together to fight evil? Yeah, right," I responded sarcastically.

"Ha! Aren't you the funny vampire tonight?"
Katie slipped her hand into mine. As we walked across
the Webster Place parking lot towards the BMW, we both
spotted Sam across the street from Pequod's pizza joint.
She was with Niklas.

"Is that Sam with Niklas?" Katie remarked,
surprised.

"Didn't she say she was going on a date tonight?"
I asked as we made our way over to Sam. Niklas instantly
sensed us and whispered something in Sam's ear. She
turned to us and waved. "Let's not scare Sam," I whispered
to Katie as we approached them.

"Okay." I knew Katie understood what I meant.

"Sam, Niklas."

"Evin, so nice to see you again," Niklas remarked
with a grin. "Hello, Katie."

"You already know Katie and Evin?" Sam asked, a
bit confused.

"I do. I used to live in a coven with Evin and I met
Katie the other day."

"Sam, you didn't mention you were going on a date

with a vampire," Katie looked to Sam, then to Niklas.

"I didn't get a chance," Sam replied, a bit defensively.

"Niklas, may I speak to you for a moment, in private?" I asked, trying to keep my tone polite, but knowing even the girls could hear an adamant note in my voice.

"Why, certainly, Evin." Niklas turned to Sam, taking her hand and gazing at her sweetly. "If Sam doesn't mind, of course."

Sam was still confused. "Uh, no . . . of course not."

Niklas and I walked a little ways down the sidewalk, out of the girls' earshot. "What are you doing, Niklas?" I demanded. "Why are you following Katie and me? Now you're on a date with her roommate? Did you really think I wouldn't find out about this?"

Niklas smiled sweetly, but he wasn't fooling me. "They are roommates? I had no idea." He turned and looked towards the girls, then back to me. "Well, that *is* interesting." He paused for a moment. "Is this how your treat an old friend?"

"We're not friends, Niklas. If you have questions for me then ask them, but leave my family and those I care about alone."

"Oh, I see. But it's okay for you to rough up my fledgling." Niklas leaned against a car parked next to him on the street.

"Look, Sam and Katie are nice girls, and they have nothing to do with what you want." I felt by body tensing up.

"And what is it exactly that I want, Evin? You seem to think I want something from you. Or that I'm out to hurt you," he replied, playing with his keys in his hand, a wicked gleam in his eyes.

This was starting to frustrate me. "You know damn well what you want. You want to know why Elli and I can walk in the sun and you can't. Well, I don't know how it's possible I can do it, either. All I know is that I can. That's all anybody knows about it, and my friends and family know exactly as much as you do, so lurking around them like some old specter in a horror movie isn't going to accomplish anything." I looked over towards the girls,

who were watching us. Katie seemed nervous. "You and I
have business to discuss at a later time, especially about
you visiting my family." I could feel my incisors starting to
come out.

"Agreed, Evin. We do have business to discuss,
though I could care less about your little family." Niklas
turned and smiled at the girls. "Until then, try to act like
a gentleman. Your true colors are starting to show." He
glanced at my incisors, then turned and walked back
towards the girls. I followed.

"Everything alright?" Katie asked, trying to cover
up her uneasiness.

"Of course," Niklas replied. "We were just catching
up." Niklas turned to Sam. "We are going to be late for our
midnight movie."

"What are you guys going to see?" Katie asked,
turning to Sam.

"*Vampire Evolution.*" She turned to Niklas giggling,
and he returned her smile.

"Are you coming home right after?" Katie asked.

"Of course, Mom," Sam retorted sarcastically.

"Don't worry, okay?" Niklas grabbed Sam's hand, pulling her along with him down the sidewalk.

"See you later, Evin," Niklas shot me a meaningful glance as they made their way across the street to the theater.

I put my arm around Katie. "It's going to be okay. I don't think he's going to hurt her."

"You don't think!" Katie turned to me with a look of horror.

"Okay, that didn't come out right. But I really don't think he will hurt her. He just wants to get under our skin. He's trying to make sure I know he's close, and that he's not going away."

"In the meantime, my best friend is going to the movies with a psycho vampire."

"Look," I grabbed Katie's hand and looked into her eyes. "We'll wait up for Sam to get home. Then we'll fill her in on Niklas so she doesn't get more involved with him than she already has." I kissed her hand. "I promise you I won't let him harm you or Sam, okay?"

"Okay," Katie leaned towards me and kissed me. "I

trust you."

"Good." I couldn't help wondering if I was making a promise I couldn't keep.

Chapter 10

"WHERE have you been? It's like three in the morning!" Katie demanded as Sam walked through the door.

"Jeez Katie, relax. The movie was over around one-thirty and we took a walk before coming home." Sam stomped into the living room and plopped down in a huff across from me. "What is the big deal?"

Katie sat down next to her. "There's something I have to tell you about Niklas." I could tell Katie was nervous about how Sam was going to react.

"Listen, Katie, Niklas told me that he and Evin don't get along." Katie looked to me as she grabbed Sam's hand.

"What exactly did he say?" I asked.

"He said that he never agreed with the rest of his coven about turning you, and that you have always resented him for that." I could tell Sam felt awkward saying this.

"This is true. He did have a problem with my sister turning me, but it's not for the reasons you may think. He was angry at the time because he wanted to completely drain me, but the rest of them wouldn't let him." Katie and Sam were both fixated on what I was saying. "Niklas was the first to bite me."

"Why did he bite you?" Katie asked.

"I was following a young lady who happened to be in his coven. She also happened to be my sister, but he didn't know that at the time. He probably claims he was protecting her and the coven, but the truth is he's a brute. He was just greedy for a meal. We all know full well that one defenseless human alone in a dark alley is no real threat to a vampire like Elli." I realized I was becoming angry.

"I just don't understand," Sam replied, confused. "Did he already know who I was when he asked me out, then?

Was this all just some kind of plot?" I could tell her feelings were hurt. I moved over to sit next to her and took her other hand.

"Listen, you're a wonderful girl. I'm sorry you got involved in all this. As your friend . . ." I squeezed her hand and looked her directly in the eyes, "as your friend, I feel obligated to tell you that Niklas is not a good character. He's angry, and he tends to act out on that anger. He has hurt many people, and he's done some really terrible things that not even the vampire community agrees with."

I was unsure just how much I should tell her. I didn't want her to be unnecessarily frightened, but I wanted to make sure she was scared enough to keep Niklas away from her.

"I understand." Sam turned to Katie. "Do you agree with Evin? Do you think Niklas is a bad guy, and that I should stay away from him?"

"I do. I trust Evin. Niklas is a very dangerous vampire." Katie gave Sam a puppy dog look and hugged her. "I'm so sorry, Sam. I'm sorry he pushed his way into your life, and that now we have to tell you these things about him. It's so unfair." I could tell Katie was hurt for her friend's sake.

"It's okay. I mean, he *is* unbelievably sexy. But he does seem a little . . . different, and not just because he's a vampire. I mean . . ." Sam looked over to me. "Evin, you seem like a normal guy." She blushed.

I laughed. "It's okay. I understand what you mean." I gave Sam a hug, then looked at her sternly. "Okay?" She nodded and I stood up. "I really need to get going. It's late." I crossed over to where Katie was sitting and kissed her on her forehead. "I'll call you later."

She looked up at me. "Okay. Be careful going home."

"Goodnight, Sam." I directed a smile towards Sam, then looked back to Katie. "Lock the door behind me."

"I will," she said.

On the way home, I couldn't help thinking about the night's events and about Katie. I had been so self-involved the last few decades that all these new feelings were overwhelming. But the one thing that surprised me the most was the intense protectiveness I felt towards Katie, especially when I thought of how close Niklas had almost managed to get to her. I knew I needed to deal with him as soon as possible. He wasn't going away on his own this time.

THE CHOSEN HISTORIAN

Chapter 11

AS Jakob and I approached the front door of Lieutenant Charles Van Vechten's warehouse on Adams Street in the West Loop, we could see two huge vampires posted at the door and several more lurking on the roof. I knew this was going to be an unpleasant visit. Charles couldn't stand me. We walked up to the two massive vampire lackeys guarding the door.

"We're here to see Charles. We have an appointment." I could feel Jakob's uneasiness as he stood beside me.

"He's waiting for you," replied one of the massive guards. He moved out from in front of the door and opened it to allow us in. "Go straight to the freight elevator and take it to the seventh floor."

I glanced at Jakob and we walked in past the guards. I scoped the area as we crossed over to the freight elevator, and another huge vampire inside the elevator opened the freight door to let us in. He acknowledged my presence by nodding slightly, but ignored Jakob. This is a common reaction to humans by most vampires. Personally, I had always felt it was a bit hypocritical for vampires to snub humans like that, especially since the formation of the Federation. They demanded that humans acknowledge us and grant us rights and protections, but did not want to acknowledge human existence themselves. I thought it was strange to act so superior to humans when in reality, vampires were trying to adapt to the human world and gain acceptance in it in every way. Maybe it was because I never thought of our unique characteristics as superior that I didn't understand this complex of theirs. As vulnerable to other species as we are during the daylight hours, what was there to feel superior about?

The guard in the freight elevator took us the seventh

floor, and we stepped out into an open area designed to be Charles's office. To the left was a lounge area with big couches, a huge flat screen TV, a pool table, and some of Charles's enforcers lounging around. To the right was a big cherry wood table used for formal meetings, and straight ahead was Charles sitting behind his huge mahogany desk.

"Come in, gentlemen." Charles remained seated. He didn't look up to acknowledge us, but continued to read the report in front of him. We approached his giant desk and stood there until we were asked to sit.

"Sit," commanded Charles. We sat down and waited for permission to speak. "So, Evin, Jakob has informed me that you have a . . . situation." Charles finally glanced up from his report, looking directly at me.

"Yes, Charles, that's right." I paused, unsure how to continue. "It's Niklas. He's back."

"Why is this a problem? From what I know, Niklas has paid for his poor decisions."

"He's here because he wants to know why Elli and I can walk in the sun. He's willing to do anything to find the reason. He went after my family, and now he has come directly to us."

"I understand his curiosity. I have always been curious myself as to why you have this special gift."

"Charles, Elli and I don't know why we have this gift, either. I'm afraid Niklas is willing to go to great lengths to find the answer. I think he wants to obtain the gift so he can use it somehow himself."

"And how are you so certain of this?" Charles rose from his huge leather desk chair and moved over to the window to look out.

"Sebastian came to visit me. He told me Niklas was obsessed with finding out how to obtain my gift." I paused for a few seconds. "Look, Charles, I understand that you and I have had our . . . differences."

"Differences? DIFFERENCES?" Charles was on top of me within a second, pinning me flat against the ground. "You kissed Laura, you little bastard! I still owe you a huge ass wiping for that. Why should I help you?" His fangs were out and inches from my face.

I groaned as he shoved my face harder into the floor, but was determined not to give up. "I come to you as my lieutenant because I am required by the Federation to report issues between myself and another vampire. I need my lieutenant to help resolve this matter. Niklas has already fed from some of my family members. He didn't kill them, but you and I both know the Federation doesn't endorse feeding from humans without their consent. Now he's in your jurisdiction, dammit! He's following me and the people I care for. I know him, Charles. I know he's willing to break vampire law to get what he wants."

Charles let go of me, regaining his composure and sitting back down in his seat. I straightened up, dusted myself off, and took my own seat. "Charles, I'm sorry about the incident between Laura and me, but please know that was just an isolated incident. I apologize, and I need your help." Charles was silent for a moment. I could tell he was thinking things over.

"What are you asking of me then? As far as what you've told me, he hasn't broken any laws." Charles took a sip of his Blue Island Bloody.

"May I speak?" Jakob spoke up.

"Go ahead, Jakob. You are a friend of the Federation."

"We understand that Niklas has not broken the law as of yet, but we believe he will. All we ask is that you speak with Niklas. Warn him that you are aware he's in your jurisdiction, and remind him what the penalties are for breaking vampire law. Given his track record, it's entirely possible that he'll break the law anyway if it's already part of his scheme, but we hope it will help if you speak to him."

Charles tapped his finger on his desk a few times, then looked to Jakob. "Alright. I'll talk to him. I'll remind him how unpleasant the penalties are for violating code. I'm sure he doesn't want to go back down *that* road again."

"Thank you." We started to get up.

Charles raised his voice sharply. "But understand this: it doesn't change the way I feel about you, Evin. I'm only doing this because it's my job to make sure vampires in my jurisdiction abide by the law. I will not have laws violated in my district, not by Niklas, not by you, and not by any other vampire." Charles looked me directly in the eye as he said this. "You both are excused to go."

****

"How do you think *that* went?" I asked Jakob as we drove back to my place.

"As good as can be expected, I suppose. Technically, he *is* correct; Niklas hasn't broken any laws . . . yet. I do worry, though. Even after Charles finds him and speaks with him, I don't think this is going to be over."

"You and I both know that. Hopefully we did the right thing telling Charles."

"I don't think it will hurt anything. It's better to keep the Federation up to date in case something does happen. You don't want to get into trouble yourself."

Jakob had a good point. I needed to be careful and make sure my butt was covered. The last thing I needed was a scrape with the Federation, especially considering the way Charles felt about me.

When we got home, Shawn and Elli were waiting up to hear the news.

"So tell me what happened! What did that jerk face Charles say?" Elli was pacing back and forth in the living room while Shawn sat patiently in his chair.

"Charles is going to warn Niklas and let him know he's got his eye on him." I flopped down onto the couch. Jakob took a seat in the chair opposite me.

"That's it? Just warn him?" Elli perched on the edge of the couch.

"That's all he can do. Technically, Niklas hasn't broken any laws yet," replied Jakob.

"So we just have to wait until he kills one of us or someone we love," Elli commented sarcastically.

"Elli, they can't punish him if he hasn't done anything wrong," Shawn responded. "Don't worry. We'll just have to be careful and stick together."

"I'm worried about Katie and her friends. He knows where she lives, and I'm sure he knows her schedule. I already caught him trying to get close to one of her roommates, which is way too close for comfort as far as I'm concerned." I shuddered, picturing the way Niklas had smiled at Sam.

"Well, I think it's time for us to meet her. We can help you keep her safe," said Shawn.

"Thanks, Shawn. You're right. I guess it *is* time for her

to meet the family."

THE CHOSEN HISTORIAN

Chapter 12

"I'M nervous, Evin," Katie said, grabbing my hand as we walked up to my front door.

"I know you are. I promise they won't bite," I responded. Katie looked at me and rolled her eyes.

"You're the funniest vampire I know."

"I'm the only vampire you know." We both giggled. As we came into the front hallway, we were met by Elli and Shawn.

"Katie, this is my sister Elli and her boyfriend Shawn. Elli and Shawn, this is Katie."

"Hello." Katie reached out to shake Elli's hand.

"Hi!" Elli brushed past Katie's hand and gave her a hug. "It's about time we get to meet you." Elli stood back. "It's been so long since Evin has had a girlfriend." Katie glanced at me, blushing.

Shawn reached out his hand and Katie shook it. "It's nice to finally meet you. Come, have a seat." Shawn and Elli led us into the living room.

"Can we get you anything to drink? We have Sprite, water, and tea," Elli asked.

"I'm fine, thank you." Katie and I sat down on the couch, while Shawn settled into his big chair with Elli sitting on the arm.

"So, you met Evin at his lecture?" Shawn asked. Elli was smiling and twirling the curls on the back of Shawn's head. She always does that when she is trying to contain her excitement.

"Yes, I went to the lecture for an extra credit assignment in Professor Jordan's class. I think I got a little more than extra credit by going." Katie and Elli both giggled.

"Yes, you did," I laughed. "You got me, along with all of

my problems."

"Oh, Evin, don't be so melodramatic," Elli scolded. She looked at Katie. "He's been like this all his life."

"Give Evin a break," Shawn reproached her playfully. "Besides, I don't think he's being melodramatic about this latest issue with Niklas." Shawn caught himself, then turned his attention to Katie. "But you don't have to worry, Katie. We'll make sure nothing happens to you."

"Thanks." Katie squeezed my hand.

Shawn quickly changed the subject. "Evin tells us that you're interested in American history, and that you're thinking about going to grad school to teach history. I have always enjoyed American history myself."

"I *am* interested in American history. I think it all stems from learning about my ancestors, especially . . ."

"Marianne?" Elli finished Katie's sentence. "It's okay, we all know she's your great-grandmother's great-grandmother. I knew her, too, when we were young. But not nearly as well as Evin knew her, of course." Everyone was silent for a moment, unsure if this was a topic Katie or I felt comfortable talking about.

Katie broke the tension, picking up the conversation as if nothing had happened. "My love of history did start with the mystery of Marianne. That time period is very fascinating to me. I'm curious about Marianne, though Evin and I really haven't talked about her since we discovered they knew each other." Katie gave me a look. I could tell she had questions, and was waiting for me to say it was okay to ask.

"Maybe I'll be able to answer some of your questions later. In the meantime, we need to talk about how to keep you safe until the situation with Niklas is handled," I remarked.

"What do you mean, 'handled'? What do you plan to do?" Katie asked. Shawn, Elli and I all looked to one another. This had to be answered delicately.

Shawn spoke up first. "Well . . . vampires live by a code. A set of laws. We must abide by these laws, or we face . . . consequences."

"And I take it you can't discuss these laws or consequences further with me?"

"Unfortunately not. But rest assured that if Niklas

attempts to act out, he *will* have to deal with the Federation. In the meantime, we obviously agree amongst the three of us that we're not going to let any harm come to you. I suggest we take shifts to make sure you're safe."

"What are you planning to do? You mean 'shifts,' like being with me twenty-four hours a day?"

"It will only be for a little while," I assured her. I knew she wouldn't like the idea of having a chaperone.

"No way! I can't have one of you with me all the time. I have school . . . a life. I can't have a babysitter. I won't have a chaperone!"

Elli chimed in. "We would only need to keep an eye on you from dusk till dawn. It's really not that bad. It will give us time to get to know each other." Elli got up from the arm of Shawn's chair and moved over to Katie's other side, sitting down on the couch and taking Katie's free hand. "It will be fun. I haven't had a sister in a long time." Katie and I both blushed.

"Look, we can just hang around outside your apartment if you don't want us in your way, and we'll stay at a distance when you're out and about," I assured her.

"You do *not* have to stay outside or follow at a distance. I'm more than happy to have any of you in my home or accompany me when I'm out. It's just that this whole situation is . . . weird, you know?"

"We know, but it will only be this way until Niklas is not a problem anymore." I kissed her forehead.

"Great!" Elli jumped up cheerfully. "I'm glad we have this figured out. Who's up for some *Vampire Within?*"

****

"You were right, Evin, your family is really nice. And you and your sister look so much alike," Katie remarked as she pushed me down on my bed. I pulled her with me.

"Well, we *are* siblings. Although that's where the similarities end."

"Oh yeah, that's it? You mean you lack her charm, humor, and intensity?" Katie positioned herself on my lap and I wrapped my arms around her.

"Well, I guess we do have a few things in common." I smiled and kissed her on lips. "How is it that you always seem to get me to rethink what I just said a moment earlier?"

"Maybe it's the Winthrop charm," Katie giggled.

"Ha ha, now who's the funniest human I know?"

"So what is it with us Winthrop girls that you like so much anyway?" I knew she wanted to get some info about Marianne out of me. I moved her off of my lap and onto the bed, getting up and crossing over to my bookshelf. "Why is it so hard for you to talk about Marianne?" she asked. "What are you afraid of? It's either that, or you're hiding something."

I turned to face her. "It's just . . . I haven't thought about Marianne in a long time, and I definitely haven't spoken of her." Katie got up and moved over to me, reaching up to gently brush my hair out of my face.

"I understand. But this is something we need to discuss and that you need to deal with." She brushed her finger along my lips. My fangs came out. "We can deal with anything together," she said, leaning in and kissing me.

"Okay, let's talk." I turned back to the bookshelf and pulled out a small chest from behind my books. I carried it over to the bed and sat down, motioning for Katie to sit next to me.

"What's this?"

"This chest holds precious memories of my human life." I opened the chest and pulled out a picture of Marianne. I hadn't realized how long it had been since I looked at that picture. I grew quiet, not realizing how lost I had been in my own thoughts until I heard Katie's voice.

"She meant a lot to you." I looked up at Marianne's great granddaughter's great-granddaughter and couldn't believe I hadn't seen the resemblance before.

"She did mean a lot to me. Marianne was the first girl I ever loved. I thought we would be together forever, even if her father didn't want us to be." I handed the picture to Katie.

"Wow, she was beautiful. I've never seen a picture of her." Katie brushed her finger across Marianne's face.

"Not many people back then could afford to have their picture taken, but as you know, Marianne's family was wealthy. You can keep the picture."

"Are you sure? I can't take your only picture of her."

"I'll always have her in my memories." I looked into Katie's eyes. "Anyway, I think it's long past time for me to start making some new memories." Katie leaned in and kissed me on the lips.

"So what happened to you and Marianne?"

"Well, I left for the war. Marianne and I wrote one another, but as time went by, we lost touch. Her letters to me got lost, like every soldier's letters. The mail system wasn't what it is now, you know. And the war took its toll on me. I eventually stopped writing altogether. I felt like I was losing myself . . ." I trailed off for a moment. "When I came home, I found out that her father had pressured her into marrying a man with a great job who came from a wealthy background. Not like me at all. My mother told me that Marianne had tried to put the wedding off, but after I stopped writing, she eventually gave in and moved on. She thought I had either died or lost interest." I pulled out my mother's ring. "As you know, I didn't die, at least not then. And I hadn't lost interest, but I had lost the girl. I regretted not telling Marianne how much I loved her before going off to war. I planned to ask her to marry me if I survived. I was going to give her my mother's ring." I handed the small canary diamond ring to Katie.

"It's beautiful. You were going to give her this ring?"

"I was. Now . . ."

"Now you can't. I'm sorry you never got to tell her how much she meant to you. And even though I feel selfish for saying so, I'm glad you never married her, or you would be my . . . my . . ."

"But I didn't and I'm not," I said quickly. She handed the ring back to me and I placed it back in the chest, closing the lid. "I am not related to you. I was just a boy that liked a girl, but then we grew up and apart." Katie put her arms around my neck and I slipped my arms around her waist. "I'm here with you now, and only you. Marianne is just a memory, but you are real. And I will tell you anything you need to know about her."

"Thank you, Evin." We kissed, and I felt her tremble in my arms. I held her as tight as I could without hurting her, then leaned back and looked at her.

"Do you like to dance?"

"Well, yes, I guess."

I got up, went over to my iPod stand, and hit play. Soft music poured of out my speakers. I turn and took Katie's hand, pulling her up into my arms. She leaned into me and we started to sway with the music. I felt like I was escaping, like we were in a new and separate world where only the two of us existed. I could feel Katie's heart beating against me.

"Evin?" Katie said without lifting her head from my shoulder.

"Yes, Katie?"

"I'm very happy . . . being with you."

THE CHOSEN HISTORIAN

Chapter 13

AS my eyes slowly opened, I was aware of tiny slivers of sunlight sneaking into the room between the slats of the blinds. Sunlight doesn't hurt me, obviously, but the first flash of daylight in my eyes in the morning is always more sharply blinding than I remember it being when I was human. I rolled over towards the wall to escape the light, and to my pleasant warm surprise, I saw Katie asleep next to me. When she felt me moving around, her eyes opened dreamily. She started to stretch, then she suddenly bolted upright.

"Evin, what time is it?"

I leaned over to look at the alarm clock. "It's 8:15 a.m. We must have fallen asleep."

"Oh shoot! I am late for class. I have an exam in Professor Jordan's class in like forty-five minutes!" She was already out of bed, scurrying around the room in a panic.

"Don't worry, I'll drive you to class." I got out of bed and peeled off my shirt, replacing it with one of my favorite button-ups. I turned to Katie, who was frantically looking for her shoes.

"I can't believe I fell asleep. Did you fall asleep? "

"I guess I did. I'm usually a light sleeper but I guess with you in my arms it's a different story." I could tell she was extremely worried about missing her exam. "I'll get you there on time. What's your exam about?"

"Shapeshifters. It's a review of last week's lectures."

"Well, no worries then. Jakob couldn't have shared much information to test you on."

Katie stopped rummaging frantically through her purse and turned to me. "What do you mean by that? Do you mean there are things we're not being told?"

Shoot. She always had a way of getting more out of me

than I had planned. "Well, let's just say there's a lot about shapeshifters that supernaturals don't even understand. I just meant they're a complex group, and they're very secretive about their nature." I turned around and headed to the bathroom to freshen up. I had to be more careful to avoid slip-ups about things I should not discuss.

We were on the interstate in minutes. As I pulled up along the north side of the lecture centers, Katie turned to me and gave me a quick hug.

"Good luck on your exam. Say hi to Jakob for me."

"Thanks. I guess I'll see you tonight."

"Yep. I'll see you at dusk." Katie jumped out of my car and hurried down the quad towards class.

On the way home, I thought of my conversation with Elli, about tracking down our family and finding out what happened to Noami. My mother had told me there was something special about the three of us. I hadn't really taken that seriously at the time. I had thought it was nothing more than an adoring mother telling her favorite child he was special, but maybe there was more to it. Maybe our mother had known something we didn't. Maybe being Daywalkers wasn't the only thing about us that was special after all. Maybe we were already "special" before we were turned into vampires. As I pulled up to the house, Elli was just getting into her slick black Audi R8.

"Where are you going?" I asked.

"Pottery class. I have to pick up Jasmine first."

"Do you think after your class we can meet up for coffee? I've been thinking. I want to talk to you about the last thing Mother said to me."

Elli looked at me curiously. "Sure. Meet me at New Wave around eleven-ish?"

"That works. See you then." Elli drove off and I went into the house. Knowing Shawn was asleep in their bedroom, I tiptoed into the den to do some internet research on my family.

I sit down with my laptop and Googled "Driscol." Of course, this brought up a list of information about me—my books, tours, interviews, and so on—and even some info about Elli. As I scrolled through the pages, I finally found what I was looking for: the name Noami Driscol. I clicked on the link. It led me to the Burlington Historical Society's

website, to an article from an old Hawkeye newspaper
dated July twenty-eighth, 1867. It was a short column
about how a young Burlington woman, my sister Noami,
had been accepted to a prestigious university in Ireland,
though it didn't say the name of the school. How funny
not to mention the school, I thought. I copied the article
into a file, then continued to search, but I found nothing
more on Noami. I decided to search my mother, Maureen
Driscol, instead. Another article in the Hawkeye came
up, her obituary, dated December twenty-third, 1873. It
said that my mother had died from natural causes, and it
acknowledged her surviving children, Conor and Molly,
along with five grandchildren. It stated that her children
Ellison, Evin, and Noami Driscol's whereabouts were
unknown.

I sat back in my chair. So my mother had died not
knowing what had happened to the three of us. I hated the
thought of how much pain that must have caused her. Then
it hit me: I knew why Elli and I had disappeared, but why
were Noami's whereabouts unknown? Hadn't she come
back for the funeral? What happened to my little sister? I

suddenly felt an overwhelming surge of anger at myself for abandoning them all so completely. I slammed my hands down onto the desk, and everything on it flew several feet into the air, tumbling back down around me in noisy disarray. Damn. What had I been thinking? Why hadn't I gone back to check up on my family? Oh yeah, that's right: because I'm a vampire.

****

"Evin, your chai latte is ready!" yelled the girl behind the counter. I walked up and grabbed my tea. "Thank you." The girl blushed and hurried off to help another customer.

I love chai tea. It's one of the few things I can digest without any issues. Vampires can eat and drink human foods and drinks, but it often does a number on our digestive system since we don't really need it for the nutritional value. Fortunately, the three things I love most—whiskey, coffee, and chai tea—seem to give me no problems. I returned to our table, where Elli was sipping her double espresso. Like she needs an espresso, much less a double.

"So I did some research online looking for leads about our family. I found out a few things." I sipped my chai.

"Oh? What did you find out?" Elli wasn't listening. She was looking behind me. I followed her gaze which, unsurprisingly, led to a couple of guys at the counter staring back at her. I turned back to her and rolled my eyes. She immediately snapped back to attention, blood rushing to her face—whether out of embarrassment or excitement I didn't know, and frankly, I really didn't want to.

I continued on with what I'd found. "I found out that on July twenty-eighth, 1867, Noami was accepted into a prestigious university in Ireland, though the Burlington paper didn't mention the name. I thought that was weird."

"Isn't July twenty-eighth Noami's birthday?" Elli fiddled with her demitasse.

"You're right. That would have been her eighteenth birthday." Was it just a coincidence? "She always said she was going to leave as soon as she turned eighteen. I guess she meant it."

"Well, I don't blame her. I know when I met Shawn I had no plans of staying in that small town either, even before I knew he was a vampire." She sipped her espresso thoughtfully, and her gaze wandered back over to the guys, who were still very much aware of her. Elli loves attention. It's something Shawn has had to learn to accept, but in the end he knows she's completely committed to him.

"The funny part is that when Mother passed away, the obituary said she only had two surviving children and five grandchildren. And that our whereabouts—yours, mine, *and* Noami's—were unknown. Ours understandably, but Noami's? That doesn't make sense. Why wouldn't Noami come back from Ireland for Mother's funeral, unless she couldn't? Didn't Conor and Molly know where to reach her? It just doesn't add up."

Now I had Elli's attention. "The obituary said they didn't know Noami's whereabouts?" She paused for a moment, looking down at the table. Without lifting her eyes, she spoke to me through our thoughts. *What happened to Mother? How did she pass away?*

I responded through our thoughts. I had figured she

wouldn't want to talk about this out loud. *The obituary said it was from natural causes. At least Conor and Molly were there for her.*

Elli looked up and spoke out loud. "But we weren't." She lifted her demitasse to finish off her coffee and shifted uncomfortably in her chair. "We have to go home after this Niklas thing is resolved. We have to reconnect with Conor and Molly's descendants. If we don't make sure they're happy and taken care of . . ." she trailed off as a red tear slipped down her cheek. She quickly wiped it away. "We have to find out what happen to Noami. It was our responsibility to make sure she was safe, and we didn't. Mother wanted the three of us to come together. Maybe Noami went to see our family on her own in Ireland when she never heard from us. Maybe she was trying to follow Mother's wishes without us."

"Knowing Noami, she was. She was a good girl. We will find out what happened to her, Elli. I promise." I sipped my chai. "In the meantime, about Niklas—" I began, but was suddenly cut short by the ringing of my cell phone. It was Jakob, so I answered immediately.

"Hello, Jakob."

"Evin. I think I know where Niklas is staying."

"How? Where?"

"Well, I've been watching the news, and there have been several disappearances of young women and men here in Chicago, particularly in your old neighborhood."

"In Lincoln Park? Why didn't I think of that? There are people missing?"

"Yes, three disappearances. Haven't you been watching the news?"

"I guess haven't been. I've really been caught up in my own world. Anyway, I'd always just assumed that the old mansion was torn down, or that maybe Sebastian might have been staying there. I didn't consider the possibility that Niklas may still own it."

"Evin," Jakob replied sternly, "if you're going to go over there, you had better be careful. It may still be daylight, but that doesn't mean Niklas isn't prepared for you to find him."

"I'll be careful," I promised. "I'm with Elli now. I'll have her stay with Katie tonight until I get there. Thanks again.

I'll keep in touch." I hung up and turned to Elli.

Of course, her exceptional vampire hearing meant she had already heard our entire phone conversation. "So you think Niklas may be staying in our old house? He's so predictable," she smirked.

"Correct. Elli, I need you to go over to Katie's before sundown and keep her company until I get there."

"But I want to go with you, Evin. I agree with Jakob. Niklas is sneaky. You shouldn't go by yourself."

"I'll be fine. It's still daylight and Niklas will be sleeping. Trust me, Elli. Just make sure you're with Katie tonight in case his fledglings are around. And *please* don't tell Katie where I am. Just tell her I have an appointment or something."

"Don't worry, I'll cover for you. There's no need to scare her, anyway, I'll be worried enough for the both of us. Just be careful and call me if you need me." She tapped her temple with her finger.

I smiled. "I will."

We got up and walked towards the door, past the same guys from earlier who were still staring at Elli. She waved and smiled at them, then looked at me and giggled. I rolled my eyes. But as we walked past the girls behind the counter, they all began blushing and giggling. I looked to Elli, who was already laughing at me. I opened the door for her and couldn't resist waving goodbye to the girls, who squealed as they waved back.

I saw that, Elli thought, sticking her tongue out at me.

Chapter 14

AS I approached the front gate of our old coven house, I was amazed. I had always assumed it had been torn down ages ago, and now I wondered why it had taken me so long to check up on it. It looked identical to the way it did when we lived there. I climbed the porch stairs and tried looking into one of the front windows, but they were covered with heavy curtains. The front door, of course, was locked. I tried every window as I walked around the side of the house, and the back door, too. All bolted. I stepped back, looking up to my old window, and something occurred to me. Back when I lived here, I had always kept my window unlocked so I could come and go without running into the rest of the coven if I didn't want to. I decided to try it.

The old oak tree I always used to get in and out of the window was still there, and as I leapt up onto the nearest branch, which had always been about ten feet up, I noticed the tree had grown slightly taller. I climbed up a few more branches, then leapt to the window sill, balancing on one foot as I tried the window. It slid open with ease and I jumped inside. I never imagined what I would see then—everything in my old room was almost exactly as I had left it decades ago, except for the handful of personal possessions I kept stashed safely away behind my books on my shelf at home. But my old bookshelf was still there across from the window, and still held most of my old books. I reached out and brushed my fingertips softly across the leather bindings, a cloud of dust motes swirling into the fading evening sunlight. A thick blanket of dust had settled on everything in the room—my bed, my dresser with its big oval mirror, my old writing table. *Nobody uses those anymore*, I thought. *Everybody has a laptop now.*

I moved through the room, amazed that so many of

the smells and tastes of my life so long ago were still on the air, things from another century I had forgotten about completely. Lamp oil. Horses' flanks steaming in the rain as their hooves kicked up clouds of wet dust in the street. Newsprint—not the way it smells now, but the oilier smell of a hundred years ago, the ink that smeared onto your fingers and clothes. These faint scents still clung to the old heavy curtains and lay settled in the carpet, swirling around me in puffs as I moved through them just like the dust motes from the bookshelf had when I touched them.

I opened the door quietly, and a puff of more forgotten scents greeted me so tangibly it almost felt like a gentle breeze on my skin as I slid soundlessly along the wall down the hallways towards the stairs. Lye soap, cast iron heavy with cooking grease and woodsmoke, traces of lead still emanating faintly from the paint on the walls underneath the ornate Victorian wallpaper. Then, suddenly, as I reached the top of the stairs, a strong, familiar smell practically punched me in the face, a smell that made my fangs pop out.

Blood.

My first thought was Katie, and every muscle in my body tensed. But I fought the urge to run towards the scent, realizing with a little guilty relief that it wasn't the scent of anybody I knew. I continued noiselessly down the stairs into the front foyer, turning the corner into the living room. Unlike my old room, the living room had been updated, with a sleek modern black leather couch and matching chairs, a polished teak floor, and a flat-screen TV. The scent of blood was getting stronger, and I crossed the living room towards the den following it. I hadn't smelled human blood in a long time, at least not human blood *outside* a human body. Vampires can detect a lot of scents humans can't, mammalian things like blood and pheromones, from inside living bodies, but the smell of human blood becomes a hundred times more intense when touched by air.

I found myself powerfully craving it. It had been a long, long time since I had been enticed to drink human blood, and I fought to suppress the thirst rising in my throat as I crossed the room. As I approached the door leading into the den the smell became overpowering, and when I passed through the doorway I found out where it was coming from.

I saw a young woman in her early twenties, naked and plastic-wrapped to a chair, slumped over unconscious. As I got closer, I could see bite marks standing out all over the exposed parts of her body, blood dripping along her neck, arms, and inner thighs. I pushed my craving for the girl's blood far down into my stomach and concentrated on not breathing. Relieved, I realized she was still alive, because I could smell and hear the blood flowing through her veins.

Great, I thought. I had to get this girl out of here, but a vampire can't just carry a naked bloody plastic-wrapped girl covered in fang marks out into the street at dusk. I instinctively pulled out my phone to dial Charles, then stopped short, remembering two important details: one, I was currently what you call "breaking and entering;" and two, the sun was beginning to set, and I had no idea how many angry vampires were about to wake up in that house. I stood stone-still and listened, and when I was sure I heard nothing but the girl's labored breathing, I dialed Jakob.

"Hello, Evin?"

"Keep your voice down," I whispered. "I have a problem, Jakob. I paid a visit to Niklas's house, and I'm afraid there's a human here, a . . . victim. She's in bad shape. They've been feeding on her."

"So I take it she was not a willing participant?"

"I seriously doubt it. What the hell should I do now? If we call Charles I'm going to get in deep shit for breaking in here, but what choice do I have?"

"We'll figure out how to handle Charles, but Evin, we *have* to call him."

Suddenly, I stiffened. I heard a noise down the hallway. "I hear something, Jakob," I hissed. "I have to go. Call Charles and tell him what's going on. He should be up now. He gets up early."

I hung up without waiting for a response, whirling around as I felt a presence closing in on me, about to turn the corner into the den. I was prepared to spring when Sebastian appeared in the doorway.

"Crap! You scared me." I breathed a sigh of relief, then immediately regretted it when the intense smell of the girl's blood hit me all over again.

"Keep it down. They are still asleep. You know how Niklas likes to sleep in."

"Sebastian, what the hell are you doing here?"

"Well, I still own this house, though I haven't been staying here myself for quite some time, as I assume you know. I thought it was about time to pay a visit and see if Niklas was here." He looked to the girl, wrinkling his nose and raising an eyebrow. "I take it he is." He circled the still-unconscious girl, and I could see the blood was getting to him, too. "She is still alive."

"Yes. And I don't think she's a willing participant in this whole thing."

Sebastian looked up at me. "Of course not. That is not Niklas's style." He smiled, his fangs out.

"Well, Jakob is calling Charles as we speak. I'm sure he will be here shortly. Maybe we should check the rest of the place out before they get here."

"Agreed. I am assuming he is still sleeping in the hidden room off the basement. I feel like I can sense him here. What I am worried about is where his little fledglings are. Niklas likes to sleep alone."

"We'll be careful, then." We moved throughout the house, not nearly as slowly and stealthily as I had when I'd been alone. We checked all the rooms quickly and reached the door to the basement within a few seconds.

"I will meet you down there," Sebastian said. And then he vanished into thin air.

Shit. I hate it when he does that. I made my way cautiously down the pitch-black staircase, although I can see perfectly in the dark. Reaching the bottom, I saw three coffins leaned against the far wall. Niklas had made the basement into a sort of horror-movie lair. He always had exquisite taste.

I could sense vampires within the coffins. Now what was I supposed to do? I had no idea where Sebastian was, and I couldn't just open the coffins. Word of advice—*never* open a coffin on a sleeping vampire. Even in our sleep, we can sense danger, and are likely to bite first and ask questions later.

Suddenly, I heard a vampire stirring in one of the coffins, about to get up. I backed away as quickly as I could without making a sound, but I was a little too slow. The coffin lid pushed open to reveal a dark-haired vampire I didn't know, and he was *not* happy to see me. He lunged at me, fangs out, fully intent on tackling me, but since older vampires tend to be faster and stronger than fledglings, I darted easily to the side and he crashed into the opposite wall.

He recovered quickly, spinning around into a crouching position with his fangs out. "What are you doing here?" he spat.

"I'm just visiting my old friend Niklas," I retorted. I couldn't help smirking. This wasn't good, but I wasn't *too* nervous—like I said, I knew I was stronger and faster than this wild new vampire, and I knew Sebastian was around somewhere even if I couldn't see him. The fledgling hissed and shifted back and forth, like he was waiting for something. I only had a second to be puzzled, though, before I felt a hand on my shoulder, and before I knew it I was thrown across the room. Apparently the other two had awoken. I hit the break wall and slid down, but was back on my feet in a fraction of a second. I turned around, slowly and deliberately sinking into a crouch. I was ready to kick some ass.

I growled. "Okay. *Now* I'm pissed."

I recognized one of the vampires as Ashton, who was alongside the dark-haired vampire who first jumped at me, as well as a redheaded girl I'd never seen before. No Niklas. Dammit. I knew I had to find him, but there was no time to worry about that now. The girl lunged first, but I deflected her midair, slamming her sideways into the wall opposite the coffins. Not a millisecond later, Ashton jumped at me, and his face met my fist with a crunch. Like I said, this wasn't *too* bad, but three to one is not the best of odds in any situation, and I suddenly felt something crack into my ribs from behind me. I spun around to see the third vampire hitting me in the side with a golf club, of all things, and I couldn't help laughing out loud. But my amusement was cut abruptly short when the redheaded girl, back on her feet in a flash, kicked me square in the chest. I flew backwards, crashing into the coffins.

I grinned. "Now, now, children, if you're not going to play fair—" I pointed to the heavy lamp on the table in the corner, sending it flying into the redheaded girl's head.

Then I looked at the coffin lids that had clattered to the floor when I crashed into them, lifting one with my mind and heaving it at Ashton, who deflected it easy enough. "—then neither am I," I finished. Every small object in the room suddenly rose from its place and flew at the angry fledglings.

I may have been stronger, faster, and much more experienced in fighting, but their speed *was* impressive, and there were still three of them. I was having a hard time keeping them all in sight due to the fact that we were all whipping around at inhuman speed. I had to hand it to Niklas—they were much better trained than I would have thought possible in such a short time. I swung at Ashton, attempting to hit him in the jaw, but he deflected my punch with one hand, swinging for my face with the other. I ducked below his arm and tried to sweep his legs out from under him and missed, as he jumped out of my grasp a split second before I had him. But as he landed, Sebastian suddenly appeared behind him, and with inhuman strength and speed he twisted Ashton's head clean off. God, I thought he was never going to show up.

"Nice of you to join me, Sebastian," I huffed, spinning around just in time to catch a fist that was meant for my face. I grabbed the dark-haired vampire's forearm and flipped him over my head and onto the couch, which smashed to pieces as he landed. Before he could move, I put both of my hands firmly on either side of his jaw, twisting and pulling with all my might. I could feel it start to give, so I placed one foot on his shoulder, my hands still tight around his head. I gave his body just the slightest push with my mind as I leaned back, and the head came with me as I moved. The girl vampire, seeing all this, suddenly turned and ran with intense speed up the stairs, out of the basement and I assumed out of the house.

I looked to Sebastian and he shook his head, already knowing what I was about to ask. "He's not here, Evin. After I vanished, I went into our secret room. I was sure he would be there, but he was not."

We both looked around at the mess we'd made. It's too bad the myth about vampires turning to ash after they've been killed is crap. In reality, all you get is dead, stinking vampire corpses, blood everywhere, and, in my case, a ruined brand-new Burberry jacket.

"Charles should be here any second," Sebastian reminded me.

We headed back upstairs to the den, where the plastic-wrapped girl was moving a little but still out of it. Just then, Charles walked into the room with a couple of his gigantic bodyguards. It would have been nice if he'd knocked, but vampires don't have to wait to be invited into another vampire's home, and Charles had never been known for his manners.

"What the hell is this?" he demanded. "What are you doing here, Evin? Are you trespassing?" He looked to me for an answer, then to Sebastian, shuddering a little at the smell of the girl's blood, his fangs coming out.

Sebastian spoke up. "He is not trespassing. I own this house, which once was Evin's home as well. And what we have here is a young girl who I do not think appreciates her current condition." He took off his jacket and covered her, moving protectively between her naked body and the eyes of Charles's huge thugs.

I gently peeled the tape off of her mouth and directed

her to look at me. She was groggy, but managed to look in my eyes as I held her chin up. "Are you okay? Can you hear me?" She nodded slightly. "Okay. Do you know where you are?"

"No," she responded, her voice was so weak it would barely have been audible to human ears.

"How did you end up here?" I asked, starting to unwrap the layers of plastic securing her to the chair.

"I got out of a cab in front of my house. The next thing I knew, I was on the ground and someone or something was sucking the blood out of my neck."

"Did you see who it was?" I asked her gently. I was almost finished unwrapping her, and Sebastian held her upright while trying to keep his jacket covering as much of her as he could. Charles and his thugs stood by, looking at her as if she were a snack. Great.

"Yes. He had blond hair and beautiful greenish-gray eyes. I think I passed out. Then, when I woke up, I was lying on a couch . . ." she trailed off, starting to cry. "They . . . they . . . they . . ."

"It's okay, you're safe now." I slid my arms under her

knees and shoulders and lifted her up, instinctively keeping her face towards my chest to protect her from the cold stares of Charles and company.

"Do you remember what day it was when you were attacked?"

"Friday," she whimpered. I held her close and carried her over to Charles, who looked to me, then to her. He motioned for one of his men to take the girl, and I reluctantly placed her in his arms, taking one of her hands in mine.

"She will be safe. We'll take her to the emergency room, and I'll have the cleaners come take care of this mess," Charles informed me curtly. The girl looked to me with wide eyes, clearly terrified.

"Don't worry. I promise nothing more will happen to you. They're going to take you to the hospital to get you medical help. Okay?" I squeezed her hand.

She nodded. "Okay. Thank you," she replied softly. She leaned her head against the big vampire's chest, letting go of my hand and fading out of consciousness again as he carried her towards the door.

"He had her for three days, Charles. He played with her
. . . they played with her . . . tortured her!" My voice rose
uncontrollably. I was infuriated. Charles just continued to
look me calmly in the eye.

"I know. He will be punished, Evin. In the meantime,
stay with your girlfriend and contact me if he shows up."
Charles started towards the doorway after his bodyguards,
then stopped, turning to face me one more time. "He *will*
be punished." Then he turned and left.

"Where could he be?" I asked Sebastian. "Why wasn't
he here with his fledglings?"

"I don't know. I thought I could sense him here, but
maybe I was sensing his fledglings, though I would think I
could tell the difference."

"Well, you have my number. If you figure out where he
is, call me." I sighed and started towards the door.

"Okay," I heard him say behind me. I turned to thank
him, but he was gone.

God, I hate it when he does that.

****

"Where's Evin? I thought he was coming over tonight?" Katie asked, surprised to see Elli on her doorstep.

"Well he was, and he will, he just had a . . . a meeting," Elli responded.

"A meeting, huh? This late at night?"

"He's on vampire time. Not all vampires can get business done during the day like we can, so he has to adjust to their schedule." Elli gave Katie a wry half-smile. "So are you going to invite me in or what?"

"Oh, yeah. Sorry. Um, come in. I forgot about that rule," Katie said, embarrassed, as Elli followed her into the living room.

"So this is your place?" said Elli, looking around. Katie could tell Elli was used to places a little fancier than this.

"Well, it's home for now, or at least until I'm done with school." Katie started towards the kitchen. "Do you want a drink?" she asked, then blanched when she realized what she had just asked. "I mean, we don't have any synthetic drinks, but we have the usual . . . soda, tea, liquor and water," she stammered as she poured herself a glass of water.

"Do you have whiskey?" Elli made herself at home on the couch, propping her feet up on the coffee table and flipping on the TV.

Katie was relieved. "Sure! I have some Scottish whiskey Tiff brought back from a trip there. Would you like some?"

"Sure. Personally, I prefer Irish whiskey, but Scottish will do."

"How would you like it?"

"I prefer it neat. Thanks." Elli continued to flip channels while Katie poured her drink.

"What's the difference?" Katie asked.

"The difference?" Elli inquired, still channel-surfing at lightning speed.

"The difference between Irish and Scottish whiskey," Katie answered, sitting down next to Elli on the couch and putting her drink down on the coffee table.

"Well, Irish whiskey tends to be distilled three times in a pure pot, while Scottish whiskey is usually only distilled twice, and they use peat smoke to give it flavor."

"Wow, you can taste the difference?"

"Oh, yes. I mean, human whiskey connoisseurs can tell these things to a degree, just like wine enthusiasts, but vampires have even sharper senses and can definitely taste subtle differences in flavors that humans usually can't. Of course, even before I was reborn, I always had a knack for being able to tell the difference between liquors."

Katie pondered this. "Um . . . I thought vampires didn't like human food and stuff?"

"It's not that we don't like them, it's just that we don't need them for nutritional value, and so they tend to upset our digestive systems. Though some of us are fortunate enough to be able to eat and drink most things without feeling bloated and nasty. "

"Oh . . ." Katie leaned back, turning her attention to the TV. "So are you looking for something? I mean, something to watch?"

"I heard there's a new reality show on TV where they have humans and vampires living together in a house in New Orleans. "

"Oh yeah, I heard about that show. It's called . . ." Katie tried to recall. "*Living With the Dead.*" They both giggled.

"Oh my God," Elli laughed. "Who thinks these things up?"

"Who knows? I heard they were pulling in huge ratings, though."

"I'm sure." Elli looked around. "So where are your roommates? Do I get to meet them tonight?"

"Well, Tiff is out of town, but I totally think you two will hit it off. And Sam has a late class tonight, but she should be home soon. We were talking earlier about maybe watching that new movie *Fallen Immortal Lover* tonight."

Elli got excited. "I've been wanting to see that movie! Shawn and Evin can be such ninnies when it comes to drama and romance." They both giggled. "May I watch the movie with Sam and you?"

"Absolutely! You can watch movies with us girls anytime. You don't have to wait for the ninnies to see it with you." They both giggled. Katie was relieved this was going so well. Elli seemed so . . . sophisticated. Katie had to admit it was a little intimidating.

"Great!" Elli hugged Katie. "You remind me a lot of our little sister Noami . . ." Elli trailed off at the thought of Noami's uncertain fate, but quickly shook it off and turned her attention back to Katie. "Although you look a lot like Marianne."

"I do?"

Elli nodded. "You do. You have her beautiful blond hair and her innocent blue eyes."

"Well, I'm not so innocent."

"Neither was she." Both girls laughed. "But she was a good girl."

"Evin really loved her," Katie said thoughtfully, though it sounded more like a question.

"Yes, he loved her very much. But they were young." Elli took Katie's hand.

"If this is too hard for you to talk about . . ."

"Oh no, not me," Elli assured her. "It's not hard at all. I mean, I wasn't the one that loved and lost." Elli paused. "If you ever want to know anything about Marianne or her family, I'm always here to answer any questions you may have, though Evin would probably be more of an authority on the subject."

Katie looked away. "I know . . . but he's made it clear he doesn't want to talk about her. I mean, he says he will if that's what I want, but I can tell it hurts him. I'd rather let it rest then hurt him."

"Well . . . what is it you want to know?'

"I want to know what her favorite book was, what she liked to do for fun, if she was a good student, if she was happy with her life after Evin . . . you know, everything."

"Well, I can't say if she was happy with her life after Evin, but I've always imagined she was. I saw her from a distance several times in Chicago before Evin and I left, and she always seemed happy. I never spoke to her, of course. I should have been a lot older than her, but you know, I didn't look it, so talking to her was kind of out of the question." Elli paused, thinking back. "Evin and I saw her once together before leaving Chicago, and I believe it was the only time he saw her after turning. We were on State Street, and she was with her husband. I pretended not to notice her so as not to be noticed, but Evin couldn't help but meet her gaze. She looked a lot older than he did, but somehow I'm sure she recognized him. They walked past each other, and I saw him turn to see if she looked back." Elli took a long sip of her whiskey.

"Well, did she? Look back?"

"No." Elli took another quick sip. "She didn't look back. And after that day, neither did Evin. Of course, I played it off and acted like I didn't see what happened. Anyway, now Evin is here with you." Both girls were quiet for a moment.

"So was she a good student?" Katie asked, changing the subject.

"She was. She was a wonderful student and wanted to go to a university, but I think her father had different plans. I'm pretty sure he wanted her to marry into wealth. She loved to read. Marianne and Evin would read in the apple orchard on her farm often after school. She loved Dickens, Shakespeare, Ben Jonson, and Daniel Defoe. She loved *Much Ado About Nothing*, *Robinson Crusoe*, *Gulliver's Travels* . . . she loved to wear the color yellow and had a wonderful sense of style for the time. She was always happy, always bright, always a lot of fun to be around. She spent her youth playing with Evin and me on her family's apple orchard, skipping rocks, reading adventure books, dreaming of her future."

"She seems wonderful."

"She was." Elli smiled. "I'm sure you have a lot of her qualities."

All of a sudden Elli's smile disappeared, and she jumped up off the couch.

"What is it?"

"Someone's here."

"It's probably Sam getting home," Katie ventured nervously.

"No, it's a vampire. I can sense him. Stay here. I'll be back." Then, abruptly, Elli vanished into thin air.

"Wow. That's different," Katie muttered to herself.

Suddenly finding herself alone in the room, she looked around, unsure of what to do. She heard the front doorknob turning, and scrambled to the closet to grab their home's only protection, a huge Louisville Slugger. She laughed quietly to herself when she thought about how little damage it would probably do to a vampire, but positioned herself next to the door anyway, waiting to swing, as the doorknob turned and the door began to open. Katie raised the bat high over her head and got ready to swing, just as Sam stepped through the door and stopped short, giving out a little yelp when she saw Katie.

"What are you doing? Katie, don't hit me!" Sam squeaked, ducking and covering her head with her purse.

Katie lowered the bat and exhaled loudly. "Oh my God, Sam, I'm sorry. I thought . . ." she paused, trying to phrase her response carefully. "I thought maybe you were an intruder."

"Uh huh," Sam nodded skeptically, shutting the door and locking it behind her. "Katie, what's going on?" She could tell Katie wasn't telling her everything. They'd known each other a long time.

"Well, Elli's here until Evin gets here tonight, and she thought she sensed another vampire around. She's checking things out right now."

"Oh," Sam paused. "Maybe it's Evin?"

"I don't think so. Evin and Elli can sense each other.

She would have known the difference."

"I would have," Elli's voice spoke up from the empty living room area. Both girls jumped as Elli's familiar shape began to materialize on the couch.

"I didn't hear you come back," Katie said as she and Sam moved to sit down.

"Yeah, well, I'm a vampire, you know. We're sneaky little things." Elli smiled, her fangs showing.

"Did you see anyone?" Katie asked.

"No, but someone was out there." Elli picked up the remote and resumed channel surfing. "Anyway, Evin is on his way home. He's going to change and get Maiko. They should be here in a couple of hours."

"How do you know that?" Katie asked.

"He called me," Elli tapped her temple with her finger.

"Oh." Katie paused for a moment before realizing she hadn't introduced Elli and Sam. "Sam, this is Elli. Elli, Sam."

"Hello," Elli spoke first.

"Hi. It's nice to meet you." Sam got up off the

couch. "Well, I'm going to go change into something more comfortable. Still want to watch that movie tonight?"

"Absolutely. Elli's going to watch it with us. She's been dying to see it." Katie caught herself, realizing what she'd just said, and both girls instantly turn to see Elli's reaction. To their relief, Elli burst out laughing, and the girls had to laugh too. Sam disappeared down the hallway and into her room.

"She's cute."

"She is. And she is very nice. One of my best friends."

"That's good. Good friends are hard to come by." Elli paused for a moment, then smiled. She turns to face Katie. "I've been *dying* to see *Fallen Immortal Lover.*"

They both giggled, and Katie rolled her eyes. "I guess you and Evin have the same sense of humor."

THE CHOSEN HISTORIAN

⌒ᒼ Chapter 15 ℭ⌒

I pulled up to Katie's house much later then I had expected. I could see the light of the TV flickering from inside the window. *What are you guys doing?* I asked Elli through our thoughts.

Finishing a sappy romance movie, she responded.

All right. Well, let me know when your movie is finished. Maiko and I are going to sit out here and enjoy the weather.

I patted Maiko on the head, and she looked up to me and smiled her doggie grin. We walked up to the front stairs, and I sat down while Maiko sniffed around the front of the house. My gaze moved up and down the street looking for anything unusual. The night's events began to replay in my mind. *What a mess this whole situation has become*, I thought. Thankfully, Charles had seemed to be understanding about everything, especially considering Sebastian and I had killed two fledglings. Immediately, my thoughts turned to the vampire girl who had gotten away. Where was she? More importantly, where was Niklas? I just knew that bastard was out there planning something nasty. Before long, Elli's thoughts snapped me out of my reverie. The movie was over. I got up and knocked on the door and Katie answered.

"Hey." She smiled, jumping into my arms and kissing me. "How did your meeting go?" She patted Maiko on the head.

"My meeting?"

Oh, I almost forgot to tell you—I told her you had a meeting, but didn't elaborate further, Elli filled me in silently.

Thanks for the heads up, I thought sarcastically. "Uh, it was longer than expected," I answered Katie out loud. I didn't want to lie, so I changed the subject quickly. "How was your movie?"

"Good! Much better than I expected." She turned around and pulled me down the hallway into the living room and onto the couch next to her. Maiko spread out on the floor.

"She's so cute! Can I pet her?"

"You'll have to ask Maiko," I replied.

Sam moved slowly to the floor next to Maiko. "Can I pet you, girl?" Of course, Maiko didn't reply—vampire dogs, however more intelligent than regular dogs they may be, still can't talk. But she did extend her head out for Sam to touch her, and Sam moved closer, scratching her ears. Maiko loves attention and loves to be petted. "I thought the movie was really good," Sam commented cheerfully.

"Well, I admit I thought it was cliché," Elli shrugged. "But then again, my own love story is a little cliché." She got up from the couch and stretched. "Speaking of my love story, I better get home to Shawn." She grabbed Katie's hand and pulled her up from the couch. "Thanks for letting me hang out with you both. Maybe we can do it again?"

Katie smiled. "Sure! You're welcome over here anytime."

"Absolutely!" Sam agreed.

"Great! Well, I'm off. I'll take Maiko home with me." Elli turned and sped out the door at top vampire speed, with Maiko right behind her. The girls were stunned.

"She always makes a grand exit," I laughed. Both girls turned to me and smiled.

Sam got up from the floor where she'd been petting Maiko and started towards her room. "Well, guys, I need to get some sleep. You two have a good night."

"Good night," we answered in unison, then looked at each other. Katie giggled and I smiled.

"Good night!" Sam disappeared into her room and shut the door.

I turned to Katie. "You must be tired, too. Do you want to go upstairs?" I couldn't help but smile. She returned the smile and started twisting my hair around her finger.

"Yes, I *am* a little tired."

I picked her up into my arms and carried her upstairs to her room in a flash, putting her down carefully on the bed.

"I can't get over how strong you are and how silent you can be."

I kissed Katie on the lips, and she wound her arms around me. I held her in my arms, careful not to squeeze too tight for fear I would hurt her. She cuddled closer to me.

"I like being in your arms. I feel so safe."

"You feel safe with a vampire?" I laughed.

She leaned back and looked up at me. "Not just any vampire. *My* vampire."

I kissed her lips again, then moved my mouth down to her throat, kissing it softly.

"Do you trust me now? Still feel safe?"

"Yes. I trust you." Then she asked me something that caught me off guard. "Do you want to bite me?"

"Maybe, but I would nev—"

She cut me off. "You can. I mean, it's okay. I want you to."

I pulled away from her neck to see her face. "You *want* me to? Why?"

"Because I can tell you want to, and I know you would never hurt me. Plus, I mean, I'm interested in finding out what it feels like." She paused for a second. "Um, what *does* it feel like?"

"Well, it's pleasurable for both vampire and human."

"Will it turn me into a vampire?"

"No. I would have to drain you to the point of death, then give you my blood, for that to happen. Which I would never do."

"You would never turn me?" She pulled away, as if this answer upset her.

"No, I wouldn't. This is not a life I would choose for anyone. I didn't choose it, it was chosen for me, though my sister meant well."

Katie kissed my lips. "Okay. But the question remains— do you want to taste me? Because I want you to."

I did want to taste her. I had wanted to since the moment I met her, but could not admit it to myself. It had been such a long time since I'd had human blood. I was terrified to take a taste.

"Are you okay, Evin? You seem like you're somewhere

else. I thought you could taste my blood if I gave you permission?"

"Sorry. Sometimes I get lost in my thoughts. Yes, I am permitted to taste your blood with your permission. It's just that I haven't had human blood in a long time." I looked into her beautiful eyes. "I *do* want to taste you, Katie." I kissed her lips, nibbled her earlobe, then moved my lips down to brush against her clavicle. "The truth is, I'm afraid to taste you. It's easy to take too much, because once we taste blood, we can't help but want more. Human blood is like a drug. Granted, it doesn't affect Elli and me quite the same way it affects other vampires. It's a lot easier for us to resist temptation. But the idea still scares me."

She put her hand behind my head, gently pushing my face towards her neck. "I trust you. I want you to taste me."

I felt her body pressing against mine, arousing both my manhood and my thirst. I could feel my fangs extend, and after hesitating for a moment, I pressed them slowly into her neck. I felt Katie's body tense up. Then, as I started to taste her, her body relaxed and she started to moan in pleasure, pushing her body against me as hard as she could. It had been a long time, but I remembered this feeling, this intense and intimate feeling of pleasure that came with drinking a human's blood directly from a warm, breathing body . . . only this time, it was better. It had been so long. I continued to take her in, and she continued to stir and moan, which only excited me more. After a few minutes of tasting her, I slowly pulled my lips away and licked the wound so the marks would disappear. Then I lifted my face to hers and kissed her deeply.

"Oh my goodness, that was amazing. Does it always feel so erotic when you taste someone?" Katie asked, still pressed against me tight.

"Most of the time," I answered. "It's always intoxicating for a vampire, but for a human, it depends on the situation. If a vampire takes blood from an unwilling human it can be scary and very painful for them. But if the human is willing, as you can see, it's much more enjoyable." I held her to my chest.

"Did you enjoy it as much as me?"

"I think I probably enjoyed it more," I laughed, kissing

her forehead.

"Ha! I doubt it." Katie tilted her face up and kissed my lips. Then she rested her head back on my chest and we drifted off to sleep.

THE CHOSEN HISTORIAN

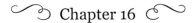 Chapter 16

I stirred in bed, confused for a moment as to where I was. It's unusual for me to feel so at peace in a place that is not my home. I rolled over to see Katie fast asleep, pressed against me. I pulled my arm gently out from under her and got up slowly, pulling the covers over her to keep her warm. I went to the window and looked out at the sun just beginning to rise. I love sunrises even more than sunsets, because sunrises remind me that I am still a part of humanity. Even though Elli and I don't belong fully to the human race, we have been able to hold on to some aspects of our human lives that other vampires have had to give up. Watching the sun come up, I reflected on the fact that I sometimes feel like I don't fit in completely with the human world *or* the vampire world.

I turned around to see Katie in bed watching me. "Well, hello. Do you see something you like?" I asked her in a playful tone.

"I do. I see a gorgeous man standing at my window." She patted the bed next to her.

I laughed and obliged, flopping down on the bed next to her. "A man, huh? I haven't been called a man in a long time."

"You *are* a man. My man." Katie paused. "Look, I may not understand a lot of things, especially how it feels to be you. But I do understand how I feel about you, and I know you're a compassionate, caring, loving being." She sat up and started curling my hair around her finger. "And you can be so charming and funny. There's nothing about you I could hate."

"Thank you. Sometimes I do struggle with my humanity, or lack thereof. It's so confusing. You would think that after more than a century and a half I wouldn't be this confused about who I am." I looked down, embarrassed for her to see the pain in my eyes. I tried to hold back, but a red tear escaped and rolled down my cheek. Katie reached up and wiped it away.

"Evin, you are gentle, thoughtful, and witty. You're more human than most humans I know. I wouldn't want you to be anybody else but you. The way you hold me and comfort me brings me such happiness. I know you say you're confused, but are you really? I think you know who you are, and more importantly, who you don't want to be. Is it really about what we are physically as much as it is the being we strive to be?"

I looked up into Katie's eyes, the eyes she shared with my first love Marianne. "You're right. I *am* the one who determines who I am." I smiled and cupped her face with my hands. "And I choose to be the man that loves you," I whispered and kissed her lips.

"Good." She smiled and kissed me back. "I love you, too." We embraced for a short moment, but to me, it felt like an eternity.

****

"I thought you were staying with Katie twenty-four hours a day?" Jakob asked, sitting down and pretending to search for something on his desk.

"Well, that was the plan, but Katie decided she didn't need a tag-along to her classes. She thinks she's safe enough during the day." I leaned back in my chair across from Jakob and put my feet on his desk. He shot me a dirty look and I quickly put them back on the floor.

"So have you talked to Charles? Has he located Niklas?" I asked, scrolling through emails on my Smartphone.

"Charles has not found Niklas." Jakob picked up a paper off the edge of his desk, looked it over, then handed it to me.

"What's this?" I leaned in and grabbed the paper.

"An email from Avery. It's about Noami."

Avery Dugan was a close friend of Jakob's from England, and also an elf. Most elves avoid the human race, though somehow they still manage to know everything that's going on in the human world. Avery is unlike any elf

I've met. He actually enjoys relationships with humans, but he's very particular and only associates with humans who are extremely intelligent and witty, like Jakob.

I looked up at Jakob studying me as I skimmed the email. I began to read it aloud: "Hello, dear old friend. I have not heard from you in ages. I am glad to hear that everyone on your side of the world is well, but I am sorry to hear about Evin's unfortunate problems with his old coven. I did some asking around about his sister Noami but have not turned up anything thus far. I did run into some fairies in Ireland that seemed to know what I was talking about, but they were wary to talk to me about Noami. In fact, they were downright rude about it, but then again, most fairies are tarts. I got the distinct impression they knew of Noami, but only Goddess knows why. Anyway, when I find out more you will be the first person I get in touch with. Until then, goodbye, my dear old friend. Avery."

"Why would the fairies act odd at the mention of my sister Noami?" I folded the email and handed it back to Jakob.

He swatted my hand away. "No, you keep it. I have

the original, of course." He tapped out his pipe and went to fill it with more tobacco. "Who knows why the fairies were weird about it? They tend to be . . ." Jakob paused, searching for a politically correct term.

"Weird. Yeah, I know. I've had my fair share of run-ins with fairies. They always seem extremely uncomfortable around me, but I know they dislike vampires. They say we're 'against nature,'" I scoffed, laughing huffily at the thought of such bizarre little creatures calling me unnatural. Fairies look a lot like exceptionally beautiful humans, with pointy ears and dark eyes, though every now and again you'll see one with bright eyes. They say those fairies are half-human, which is extremely rare.

"I guess I do have to agree with them on that one. Vampires are not very . . . natural. But at the same time, they definitely give us a run for our money in that department."

"Regardless, you're about as natural as they come, Evin. You have more humanity in you then most humans." He lit his pipe and puffed away.

"You're the second personal to tell me that today."

I got up and stretched. "I thought you were prohibited from smoking on school grounds. Isn't there a law about smoking on or near public property?"

"Humphh. That silly law does not apply when nobody knows I'm doing it, and especially not in my own office." He took another long puff.

I smiled. "Okay, you win. But one of these days, that tobacco is going to kill you."

"Yeah, well, when that happens, I'll be ready to go."

Such a grumpy old man he's becoming, I laughed to myself, remembering the naïve little kid he had been when I met him. I started towards the door.

"Where are you going?"

"I'm going home to work on my book. I'll call you later." I turned and headed down the hallway. Several girls giggled as I walked by and I couldn't help smiling. Then I immediately thought of Katie, and texted her before I took off on my motorcycle.

I miss you. Heading home to get some work done. I'll meet you at your house before sunset. Be careful.

I realized with a little surprise and embarrassment that

I was fiddling anxiously with my jacket, rearview mirror, cell phone—anything that would give me an excuse to wait for her to text me back before taking off. This girl really had me wrapped around her finger. I was relieved when she buzzed back almost immediately.

I miss you too. Get some work done and don't worry about me. I can't wait to see you tonight. Muah.

****

When I got home, I went directly to the fridge and pulled out a bottle of Animus, downing it in one gulp.

"Is it *that* good? When are you ever going to learn to sip instead of gulping? Your manners are so gross," Elli chastised me as she planted herself on a stool at the counter.

"Never, I suppose. What do you have going on today?" I crossed the kitchen and sat down next to her.

"Nothing, really. I thought you were going to stay with Katie all day?"

"She didn't feel she needed me tagging along with her to her classes. Of course I don't like it, but what can I do? She knows he's only awake at night."

"But he could have someone else grab her during the day," Elli said distractedly, playing with her Smartphone. It was the same one as mine. The older we got, the more alike we became. It was almost ridiculous.

"True, but you know as well as I do that he hates other supernaturals almost as much as he hates humans. I think she'll be okay," I answered unconvincingly, getting up to rinse my bottle out in the sink and throw it in the recycling can. "I'm going to attempt to start on my next book today, and then meet up with Katie before sunset."

"What's your next book about?"

"It's about a wizard and a fairy that fall in love. Another commercial book." I leafed through the mail on the counter. "But Kara's pressing me for another fiction book. However, I have another historical book in mind."

"Oh, do tell." Elli put her phone down and leaned in on her elbows, intrigued.

"Well . . ." I sat down next to Elli. "You know how my last book was about vampires and their impact on the Roaring Twenties?"

"Yeah."

"Well, I want this to be sort of a sequel, but instead of talking about flappers, vampire hitmen, and smuggling booze, I want it to be about how vampires influenced Chicago and Illinois politics, as well as how we were major influences within the syndicate."

"You know, you may have some unhappy vampires on your hands with that one, but I love it. Screw Charles and the others."

"Yeah, I've been wondering how to go about writing it to minimize the outrage, but I'll figure it out. In the meantime I need to start working on my next novel before Kara strings me up." We both laughed. I kissed Elli on the forehead and then sped up the stairs to my room.

I looked at the small doggie door built into my west wall that led to a little cubbyhole where Maiko lies around during the daylight when I'm not around. I felt terribly guilty for not spending very much time with Maiko over the last few weeks, but then again, Maiko and I had eternity to spend together. Katie and I only had . . . what, fifty years if we were lucky? I hadn't had to think about that situation in a long time. Never, really, when I thought about it. I knew when I became a vampire that any thought of being with Marianne was over. Yeah, there had been women over the years, but never anyone that I thought about being with long-term. Now, here I was with Marianne's seventh great-granddaughter, of all the people in the world, who I was contemplating having an actual relationship with. A relationship with someone I would have to see grow old and die, while I remained unchanged for centuries. Shit.

I sank into my desk chair, sighing as I turned on my laptop. How the hell was I supposed to focus on a story when my own story could never end happily-ever-after? I looked at the blank screen for a moment, and then I started to write. Inspired or not, I can type five times faster than a human writer, which definitely helps when you have deadlines like mine and an agent breathing down your neck. *Screw it*, I thought, *if I can't have a happily-ever-after story, at least my characters can*. They could have the perfect future Katie and I would never have. *Bastards*, I thought bitterly, typing away. I didn't pause until Maiko slid up next to me and started rubbing her head against my leg. I tore my eyes from the screen and looked down to scratch her between the ears.

"Good morning, girl." Wait, was Maiko up? "Oh shit!" I yelled out loud, leaping from my chair. "I'm supposed to be at Katie's!" I rushed down to the living room where Elli was lounging on the couch, Maiko a millisecond behind me.

"What are you doing here?" Elli exclaimed. "I thought you would be at Katie's by now."

"I'm supposed to be. I lost track of time. Dammit! I can't drive there, it'll be too slow. I'm just going to run. I'll call you if I need you." I tore out of the house, Maiko on my tail.

We took off down Damen Avenue so fast humans couldn't see us. We ran past Six Corners, through Wicker Park, the Ukrainian Village, across West Town, under I-290 and finally into Little Italy, arriving at her door in minutes. I knocked loudly. No answer. Maiko began growling, the fur on her back prickling up.

"Katie? Katie!" I yelled through the door. Still no answer.

I threw my shoulder into the door and it clattered open. I really only needed to nudge it, but I was too frantic to care. I ran down the hallway to the living room, which, to my horror, was completely trashed. Tables were overturned. Books, DVDs, and knick knacks were strewn everywhere, and a couple of the couch cushions were torn open. The TV looked like the screen had been kicked out, and because it had somehow been switched on, it gave off a loud buzzing sound and an awful burning-electronics smell. I ripped the plug out of the socket as I ran to check all the rooms downstairs. They were in a similar condition, and there was no sign of anybody around, so I sped up the stairs to Katie's room. I could already smell the blood as I neared the top of the stairs, and as I rushed through the door I saw a girl bound and gagged on the floor. *Not Katie,* my acute senses of smell and taste told me, and it felt like my stomach had dropped into the pit of my abdomen. *If this isn't Katie,* I thought, *it means they've taken her. Oh God.*

I knelt down next to the girl and turned her gently over. It was Sam. Her face was bloody and beat up, and her shirt was torn at the collar. They had fed on her. I took the cloth out of her mouth and quickly untied her hands. "Sam, are you okay? Where's Katie?" I tried to ask calmly. *Elli, come now. They have Katie.*

"Oh Evin, they took Katie," she squeaked, her voice quavering. "They took her. And the red haired girl . . . she drank my blood. They took her, Evin. They took her," she repeated, beginning to cry.

I pulled her close to me. "It's okay, you're safe now. Elli is on her way." I stroked her hair, trying to calm her down, but I knew from personal experience how terrifying a vampire attack is for a human. "Who took Katie, Sam? How many were there?"

She swallowed and tried to breathe more slowly. "It was Niklas and that redhead. I think that was it. I didn't see anyone else, but I really don't know."

I picked Sam up and carried her downstairs. As I made my way over to the couch, Elli sped through the broken front door. Shawn stopped just short of the doorway, and Maiko barked a greeting, looking up briefly from sniffing through the rubble on the floor.

"Sam," I asked, "could you invite our friend Shawn in? He's here to help."

She glanced at the door. "Come in," she murmured.

"What happened here? Where's Katie?" Shawn asked immediately as he stepped through the door and moved into the living room.

"Niklas has Katie." I responded, surprised at how calm I sounded.

Elli sat down next to Sam and brushed her hair out of her face. "Are you okay?" Sam hugged her, choking back tears again.

"Yeah, I'll survive, I think," she said, rubbing the rope burns on her wrists.

"How did they get in?" Shawn asked.

"Niklas came in through the front door. Then he made me invite the redheaded vampire in."

"How was Niklas able to come in?" he demanded.

Sam looked confused. "What do you mean?"

"Vampires have to be invited in, Sam," Shawn explained. "That's why he forced you to invite the redheaded vampire. But how did he get in himself?"

"Well, I guess he did meet me here when we went on that date, and I invited him to wait for me inside then. But that was last week. Would it still count?"

"It would. Once you invite a vampire in, they can come in any time they want until you revoke the invitation," Elli explained.

"I didn't know," Sam wailed. "I'm so sorry. This is all my fault."

"No," I said, "it's not your fault, Sam. It's mine. I should have asked you about it the night I saw you with Niklas so you could revoke it then. How could you be expected to know something like that? I'm so sorry, Sam."

"It's okay, Evin. God, I can't believe I could be so dumb. Please, just get Katie back from that jerk Niklas and that bitch of a redhead." Sam was still crying, but now her face was more angry than terrified.

Shawn knelt down next to her, resting his hand reassuringly on her knee. "Did you hear them say anything that you think might help us find Katie?"

"Yes. The redhead wanted to kill me . . . that bitch. But Niklas told her no."

"Why?" I asked, pacing nervously around the room.

"Because he wanted me to relay a message to you."

Shawn and Elli's heads snapped up to look at me. "What

did he want you to tell me?" I asked slowly.

"He wants you to meet him tomorrow night after sunset. He said you would know where to meet him, and . . ." Sam's voice faltered.

"And what?" I pressed her.

"He said . . . not to be late or he'll kill Katie like he killed your sister Noami," she sobbed.

"No!" Elli screamed, jumping to her feet. Her face was frozen and inscrutable for a moment, and then red tears began to spill down her cheeks. She buried her face in her hands, sinking to the floor. Shawn turned to wrap his arms around her and Maiko gave up exploring to sit down forlornly at her side.

I must have been crying, too, because the room looked red. I heard a scream of rage coming from somewhere behind me and whirled around to see who the hell it was, surprised for a moment to come face to face with nothing but a blank wall. I blinked at the wall for a moment, dumbfounded.

Then I realized the screamer was me.

I slammed my fist through the wall, punching a huge hole. A couple of pictures still dangling crookedly on the wall crashed to the floor and I heard the tinkle of breaking glass. Maiko barked. I pulled my fist out and turned around, still screaming. "I'll kill him! I'll kill that son of a bitch once and for all! I can't wait till tomorrow! I'm going after Katie now."

Shawn stood up. "I know you're upset, Evin. We all are. But please, let's think about this first. We have no idea where he is or how many vampires are helping him. He could even have other supernaturals working for him," he put his hand on my shoulder and looked intently into my eyes. "Do you understand? We need to figure out where he's going to be at sunset, and we need to get help."

Elli stood up too. "Shawn's right. We have to keep our wits about us." She wiped her eyes and put her arms around me. *We will find her. We're in this together.*

"Okay," I said, managing to compose myself. "Shawn, you call Charles and tell him what happened. Elli, help Sam get cleaned up."

"What are you going to do?"

I patted Maiko on the head. "I'm going back to our old coven house to retrace my steps. I have to figure out where this place is that Niklas wants to meet."

THE CHOSEN HISTORIAN

 Chapter 17

"EVIN will find me, and he'll kill you!" Katie screamed.

Niklas only chuckled. "My dear, he will never find us here because he has never been here. I bought it long after he had left our coven, right before the World's Fair of 1893. Have you even heard of the fair?" Niklas turned his back to her, playing with his ring.

"Of course I have. It was the greatest fair in the world."

He turned to face Katie, who sat tied to a chair in the middle of the room. "You're right. It was the most beautiful fair in all the world. People came from every corner of the globe, and it was the biggest playground I ever had." He smiled gruesomely, showing his fangs. Then he spun back around. "It was truly an amazing and magical place for everyone, especially me."

"What's your point?" Sweat dripped down Katie's temples.

Then she gasped—in less than an instant, his face was inches from hers. "It was in this house that I murdered all those young women and men during the World's Fair." He smiled wickedly. "I would meet them, charm them, seduce them . . . then bring them back here and eventually kill them." He stood up and began to pace the room. "You see, I love the hunt almost as much as the kill."

"You're a monster!" she screamed

Niklas laughed. "That I am. A monster who is going to kill your boyfriend. Once I drink his blood, no one will be able to stop me. I will be not only an animal of the night but of the day as well. I will kill the elders for daring to punish me in the past, and I will make my own army of fledglings who will help me rule the world. We will make humans our slaves, as they should be."

"You're a foul, disgusting creature! Evin will never

let that happen," Katie spat, her anger helping hold back hysterics.

"Oh, but he will. He will let me feed from him because of you." Niklas laughed.

"No, he won't. I won't let him sacrifice himself for me."

"But you have no choice." Niklas walked towards the door, but stopped and turned. "See you tomorrow night, princess. Say your prayers while you can." Then he walked out of the room and slammed the door.

****

The sun would be rising soon. What the hell was I going to do? I had to figure this out. Niklas was so predictable, I *knew* I had to already have the answer. It was just a matter of putting together the puzzle.

Maiko and I wandered through the old coven house searching for clues. My cell phone rang.

"Jakob. Have you heard anything? Have you been able to locate Sebastian?"

"No, I can't find him. Unfortunately, I don't think we

will until he is ready to be found."

"I know. You're right. I was hoping Sebastian would help us, but now I don't know if that's going to happen. Even if we *could* find him, there's no way to know for sure that he'd help us. He knows Niklas is a monster and he doesn't approve of the things he's done, but he's still in love with the bastard."

"Well, we may never know the answer to that. But if Sebastian does show up, I sure hope he's on our side."

"Me too."

"How is the search of the old home going? Find anything?"

"No. I can't think straight. I'm so angry I can't focus." I kicked a dusty old trash can across the room. Maiko jumped, shot me an annoyed "harrumph" and continued to sniff around the room.

"You *must* focus, Evin. Katie's life depends on it."

"I know, I know." I felt myself shaking with anger. "I can't let that bastard hurt her."

"Then focus, Evin. He said you would know where to find him. When you were a coven, was there a place you all loved to go together, or maybe somewhere he liked to hunt?"

I thought about this for a moment. "We really weren't much for hanging out together." I paused. "Wait . . . the night he tried to kill me and Elli stopped him, it was . . ." I tried to remember what street we had been on that night. "In the alley outside that old warehouse off of Washington and Clark. Sebastian and Niklas owned that old warehouse. It's where they kept some of their valuable antiques, and where Niklas would take a lot of his victims. But that place *can't* be there anymore. I'm sure they tore it down and built some high rise long ago. The court house is right near there."

"I'll do some research and find out what I can about the old place, and see who owns the property now. In the meantime, go home and get some rest. You won't do anyone any good if you're weak."

"You know I don't need much sleep."

"But you do need blood. Or at least the synthetic stuff. So go home. I'll call you when I find something new."

"Okay." I hung up. *Jakob is right*, I thought, *I need my*

strength. Niklas was a lot older than me and he still drank human blood, which gave him an advantage over me. Surviving the way I did off of animal and synthetic blood, I wasn't as strong as I could be.

I sighed. "Maiko, let's go home."

****

As soon as I walked in the door, Elli jumped up and started firing off questions. "Did you find anything out?"

"No, but I think I know where he might be. Jakob is doing some research for me right now."

"On what?" asked Shawn from his favorite chair in the corner.

"That old warehouse that Sebastian and Niklas owned back in the 1860s."

"Yes, the place where you were reborn," Shawn said thoughtfully. "How could we have forgotten about that? It was Niklas's favorite place to take his victims."

"And it's where I wouldn't let him kill you," Elli commented. She stopped pacing and allowed herself to sit down on the couch.

"And the place he plans to finish what he started, I suppose." I replied. "But it won't happen. I won't let him hurt Katie." I sat next to Elli and took her hand.

"You sound as if you're planning to go by yourself," Elli remarked, but it sounded like a half-question.

"Of course. I can't ask the two of you to put your lives at risk for me."

"What? Are you kidding me? I didn't let Niklas kill you the first time, and I'll be damned if I'm going to let him try it now." Elli's voice became stern and motherly. "Evin Shannon Driscol, I will *not* have you fighting this fight without your big sister."

"But . . ."

"But nothing. You and Shawn are all the family I have left. Besides, we're stronger together than apart."

"The three of us *are* stronger together," Shawn agreed. We both turned to look at him, surprised. "Well, you don't think I'm going to let the both of you get killed, do you? You're my best mate, Evin, and Elli is the love of my life. We fight together."

"Together," Elli repeated.

"Together," I affirmed. We all grew silent for a moment. "So how's Sam?"

"She has some bumps and bruises, but she's going to be okay. We put her on the Metra to her mom's house and she's going to stay there until all this is over," Shawn answered.

"Well, good. With both roommates out of town, we have one less thing to worry about. What did Charles say when you talked to him?"

"He said to call him when we figure out the location and he'll be there."

"Now we just have to wait for Jakob to get back to you about the old warehouse."

"I know." I leaned back and sighed. "I hate waiting."

⌒☽ Chapter 18 ☾⌒

"WHERE are you?" demanded Jakob when I answered his
call. He could undoubtedly hear the wind whipping past
my Bluetooth earpiece as I sped down Clark Street on my
bike.

"I'm on my way to Washington and Clark."

"I thought you were going to wait to hear back from
me."

"You know me. I'm not a patient man."

I pulled my motorcycle into the alley off of Clark.
Here was another place I hadn't been back to since the
day it changed my life forever. The alley was, of course,

completely different, with up-to-date fire escapes so unlike the rickety ladders of the nineteenth century, electric lights, and modern signs outlining exactly when and where not to think about parking; but it was still strangely the same. The buildings were different, but the shape of the alley, the way the shadows played off the buildings, even traces of scents here and there all took my mind back to that day in 1866 when Niklas had jumped me. It was funny when I thought about how that day seemed to have come full circle now as I got off my bike and started looking for a way in.

"Be careful," Jakob reminded me. "The sun is going to set soon."

"Did you find anything out?"

"Yes. The building changed hands several times after Niklas and Sebastian owned it, and eventually was torn down and replaced by the building you see now. It now belongs to a big developing corporation that owns several pieces of prime downtown real estate. I can look into it if you want, but I seriously doubt Niklas has any connection with the company. If anything, he's just diabolically fixated on the location. "

I looked up at the high rise that now towered over the place where the old warehouse once stood. "No, don't bother. I figured that would be the case. Anyway, I wanted to get down here to search the area before Charles and his crew arrives. I'll keep you posted." I clicked off the earpiece, stashed it in my pocket, and walked quietly along the wall and up onto the loading dock. I tugged on the door, but it was locked. No problem. I yanked harder and the heavy deadbolt snapped, the door swinging open. I waited anxiously for an alarm to sound, and to my relief, nothing happened. *It's a good thing we only need an invitation to enter a residence,* I thought, *or we'd never get anything done.*

My footsteps echoed down the empty hallway that led into a deserted lobby. *This doesn't feel right,* I thought uneasily. I had no idea where to start searching this building. The only connection Niklas and I had to the building was that I had been reborn in the alley, and I really couldn't begin to guess what else about the location would have any special significance to him.

Evin, said Elli through our thoughts, *Charles is on his way. Shawn and I just pulled up in the alley.*

Okay. I'm in the lobby.

Suddenly, my cell rang. It was an unknown number. "Hello?"

"Evin."

My fangs shot out. "Niklas. Where are you? Where is Katie?" I spun around to check my surroundings.

"Are you down off of Clark?"

"Yes. What the hell have you done with Katie?"

"I knew you would go there. You are so predictable. Are you alone?"

"Yes."

"You answered too fast. Are you alone, Evin? Don't make me punish Katie for your mistake."

"I'm alone . . . now, but I won't be for long. Charles and his crew are on the way."

"Oh, Charles. That old bastard. I never liked that sorry excuse for a vampire."

"I'm sure it's mutual," I answered drily. Niklas laughed. "What now?" I asked.

"I want you to lose the posse. Slip out and meet me alone."

I hesitated. This was obviously a trap, but I couldn't see a way out of it that left Katie alive. "Okay. Fine. Where do you want me to go?"

"Find a way to get out of there unnoticed. Then head to U.S. Cellular Field."

"And do what?"

"Just do as I say." Niklas hung up abruptly.

"Shit!" I spat out loud.

"What's wrong?" I heard Elli's voice behind me. I turned to see Elli, Shawn and Maiko emerging from the hallway into the lobby.

My thoughts wanted to scream, *Elli, help me*, but I forced them to stay quiet. She couldn't know—she couldn't follow me, or he'd kill Katie. "Oh, nothing," I sighed. "Just flustered."

"Don't worry, Evin. We'll find her."

"I know. Listen, why don't you guys check the fifth through the tenth floors, and when Charles gets here he can check the floors above that. I'll go check the lower level and work my way up."

"Okay," Shawn nodded.

"We'll meet back here if we don't find anything," I said. Elli and Shawn headed for the stairwell door. I pretended to sniff out the lobby until I was sure they were gone.

"Okay, Maiko, time for us to get Katie." We ran back out into the alley. "Well girl, we can't take the motorcycle, can we? There's nowhere for you to ride. I guess we'll just have to run. Are you ready for a run, girl?" Maiko wiggled her tail.

We took off down Clark Street to Monroe, then cut over to Halsted and headed for U.S. Cellular. The evening was cloudy and darker than usual, and there weren't many people out along Halsted—not that they would have seen us. We sped through Greek Town, past UIC, through Pilsen and into Bridgeport, arriving in front of Gate B at U.S. Cellular Field in less than ten minutes.

"Now what?" I muttered. Maiko strutted off to check things out. I hovered outside the locked gate, wondering if I should break it open or try to find another way in. There was no *way* the Cell didn't have a security system. Before I made up my mind, however, my phone rang again. Niklas's voice sounded amused.

"You didn't think I would actually be at the field, did you? You know I can't have that sister of yours following you, and I doubt you're strong enough to keep your thoughts to yourself."

"Stop playing with me," I snapped. "Let's get this over with."

"You were never any fun. Your next stop is Sixty-third and Morgan. The address is 6250 South Morgan. You had better be alone, Evin."

"I will. And Katie had better be all right, or—"

"Or what?" He cut me off, chuckling. "You'll kill me? I don't think so. You know I have the upper hand here. Get here, and get here soon, ol' boy." He hung up before I could say anything else.

"Shit!" I yelled, and my voice echoed across the expanse of concrete surrounding the stadium. "I'm going to kill that prick!" Hearing my voice, Maiko ran back to me from around the side of the stadium. "Let's go, girl."

We took off down Halsted, crossing over to Morgan

Street and heading towards Sixty-third. We slowed in
front of a vacant lot just as we approached Sixty-second.
I wanted to walk the rest of the way to check out our
surroundings. It was a rundown neighborhood and no one
was out. At least, no one human.

Maiko began to growl. "It's okay, girl," I reassured her,
but I knew she wouldn't have done that without a good
reason. She may not be big, but she's definitely smart. I
looked up to see several vampires emerging from behind
the surrounding houses, staying in the shadows. Shit,
there had to be at least six of them I could sense, although
I noted with some relief that they all smelled like young
vampires.

Maiko and I continued towards the house next to the
vacant lot. Unlike the other ramshackle houses on the
block, this one had fresh paint, a new-looking porch, and a
smooth concrete driveway.

We walked up onto the porch, and I whispered to
Maiko so quietly that even a vampire couldn't hear me
unless he was standing next to us. "Maiko, guard the
house. Don't let any of those vampires in. It's just you and

me, girl." I patted her, and she rubbed her head against my leg. Then she turned around and growled, showing all the vampires her fangs. "That's my girl." I turned around and attempted to open the door as quietly as I could, bracing myself instinctively for the invisible-wall feeling of trying to enter a human abode uninvited, and felt . . . nothing. I steeled myself as I stepped through the door unhindered. This could only mean one thing.

I was in a vampire's house now.

And from the smell of it, Niklas was waiting for me.

THE CHOSEN HISTORIAN

Chapter 19

Where the hell are you, Evin? Elli's voice rang out in my head over and over. *Why aren't you answering me? Evin?*

It was only a matter of time before she figured out I had left. I had to fight the urge to answer her. She couldn't find out where I was until I knew Katie was safe. I looked around the dark living room. It was well-kept but simple and sparsely furnished.

Niklas was leaning against the door frame on the other side of the room. The red-headed vampire girl was standing behind him, smirking.

"Hello, Evin."

"Where's Katie?"

"Now, now, let's not be so hasty. Have a seat?" He motioned to a few small chairs situated around a low table.

My fangs shot out. I lunged at Niklas, reaching for his throat, but he quickly sidestepped me and I crashed into the wall, leaving a web of cracks in the plaster. As I hit the floor, he redhead kicked me in the side and I flew across the room crashing into the opposite wall and thudding to the floor.

"Evin, you're going to lose this game. You know I am stronger than you. Hell, Anastasia here is stronger than you, even if she is younger. She loves to drink human blood, unlike you, you pathetic, weak little bookworm."

It was with a little difficulty that I jumped to my feet, but I tried not to show it. "Listen, what are we doing here? What do you want from me, Niklas? Let's get this over with."

Niklas rushed at me and pinned me against the wall. His hands closed around my throat, his fingernails digging into my skin and his fangs extended inches from my face. "Enough!" he roared. "Don't try to play stupid with me!

Don't insult my intelligence. You know what I want. I want to know why you can walk in the sun. Why are you so special? What makes you the chosen one, historian? WHAT?" Niklas let go of my throat, slamming me into the wall and stalking across the room.

"Are you scared, historian?" Anastasia smirked at me. She was standing a little too close for comfort, so I reached out suddenly and hurled her across the room. She hit the wall, and chunks of ceiling plaster fell down around her.

Niklas laughed. "I told you not to underestimate him, Anastasia. He may not be very strong, but he is smart as hell."

"At least you haven't forgotten that, you meathead. Maybe you'd be smart too if you spent a little time trying to learn from humans instead of just torturing them. And to answer your question, I don't know why I can walk in the sun. Nobody does. But you seem to think you do, so why don't you tell me why I have this gift?"

"I told you not to mock me, you little piece of shit!" he screamed, starting towards me again.

"Niklas, I tell you I don't know! Feeding off me won't

help, either. Look at my dog—I turned her, Niklas. I gave her my blood, and she is unable to go in the sun."

"Maiko is a dog, not a human." Niklas paused in an effort to compose himself. "It's really too bad you completely abandoned your family. If only you would have bothered to find your sister Noami, she could have told you. She knew everything." Niklas smiled wickedly.

"What do you mean she knew? Noami knew nothing of me becoming a vampire. I haven't seen my sister since 1865."

"Oh, she knew you were a vampire. She knew everything, Evin. She kept tabs on you and Elli until I caught up with her. And then . . . well, let's just say she's not keeping tabs on anyone... anymore."

"What did you do to her, Niklas? Your issue was with me!" I lunged at him, but Anastasia knocked me backwards. The room was turning red again, and I fought back tears of rage. I was going to kill this son of a bitch.

"But I couldn't find you, so . . ." He paused, turning to Anastasia and nodding his head. She began to move slowly towards me.

"First, I fed on your family, but I noticed no changes. But don't worry, I tranced them before I left. They never knew what bit them." He smiled his wicked smile. He moved around towards my right side while Anastasia circled towards my left. "I was about to give up on the family idea, but then your mother told me everything. I heard her say herself that you, Elli, and Noami were special. Did you know your mother talked in her sleep? No, probably not. You didn't bother to find out very much about her at all before you abandoned her, did you?"

"How do you know what my mother said in her sleep? What did you do to her?" *The obituary said natural causes*, I told myself. *He couldn't have killed her. He couldn't have. Could he?*

"The last night I was in Burlington I decided to go back to the house one more time. I'd already been invited, so I let myself in. Your mother kept a small box of your things under her bed—just trinkets, papers, school records, nothing interesting, but I wanted to look through them one more time. That's when I heard dear old Mom talking in her sleep. She kept repeating something, something about how the three of you were different. The funny thing is that until then, I never even knew you had a sister named Noami. To think I might never have met her." Niklas and Anastasia drew nearer, closing in on me.

"So I tracked her down and found her at her school in Dublin. Your sister was beautiful. I first noticed her in one of her late night classes. Of course, you know I prefer boys, but your sister, well . . ." he licked his lips, "she was gorgeous." He paused to reflect. "She knew what I was the moment I introduced myself. Of course, that was before the stupid Federation came along and screwed everything up, and we were still kept a secret. I couldn't let her expose me. So I knew I had to take care of her."

"What did you do to her, you bastard?"

"Unfortunately, nothing much. I never got a chance to taste her blood." His smile turned into a low growl. "The fairies got involved. They found out I was in town somehow. By the time I snatched your sister I was surrounded by half the fucking fairy Court, though I am not sure which one." I knew what he meant—he couldn't tell the Seelie and Unseelie Court fairies apart.

"Why were they there? Were they following you?" If
they had been, they certainly hadn't finished the job. God,
why were fairies such flakes?

"They weren't following me. They were following your
sister."

"What? Why? What did they want with her?" By this
point, I had completely forgotten about Anastasia behind
me.

"Fuck if I know. All I knew was that they were
interested in her, not me, but they *did* want me out of the
picture. You know how fairies hate vampires. I couldn't
shake them . . ." Niklas moved so close to me his lips were
millimeters from my ear and spoke slowly and deliberately,
". . . so I pushed her off the Cliffs of Moher."

"No human can survive that fall!"

He took a step back and laughed. "Exactly. After I
pushed her, most of the fairies went over the cliff after
her and the rest attacked me. I barely made it out alive.
Unfortunately, I never had the chance to try her blood, but
it doesn't matter. Because I finally have you."

I felt blood tears streaming down my face and didn't

bother to fight them. "What do you want from me? Please, just take it, and let Katie go." My will to fight was leaving me.

"Anastasia, please bring Katie up from the cellar."

"But—" she started to protest.

"But nothing!" Niklas roared. "Do as I say and bring the bitch up. I want her to see what happens to her boyfriend." Anastasia turned on her heels and disappeared down the basement steps.

"So this is what's going to happen, Evin. I am going to feed from you, and once I am done, I will let her go."

"Why should I believe you? How do I know you're not going to kill both of us?"

"You don't. That's a chance you're going to have to take. And it does not look as if you have much of a choice, now, does it?"

Anastasia emerged from the staircase pushing Katie in front of her. Katie held her hands together in front of her, and I could see her wrists were tied and her right eye was bruised. She'd obviously been fighting them every step of the way.

"Evin! Evin!" She tried to pull away from Anastasia, who pushed her to the ground and slapped her across the face.

I leapt at Anastasia but Niklas shoved me back across the room. "Now, now, Evin. Don't get ahead of yourself. You give me what I want, and I will let her go."

"Fine."

"No Evin, don't do it!" Katie yelled. "He's going to kill both of us. Don't let him feed on you!" Anastiasia kicked her in the ribs and I heard a crunch. God dammit, they could kill her in a second.

"Katie, please, don't say anything more. Get on with it, Niklas."

Niklas moved toward me, grasping my chin in his hand and shoving my head sideways. I could feel his lips against my neck, and then the prick of his teeth.

"Niklas, STOP!" demanded a familiar voice.

Still holding me against the wall, Niklas turned his head away from me to see his old master, Sebastian.

"Sebastian. I thought you'd never show up."

"Niklas, let him go," Sebastian demanded calmly.

Now that Sebastian was here, I called for backup.

Elli! My mind practically screamed. *6250 South Morgan.
Hurry! And bring Charles and his bodyguards. I counted
at least six vampires outside.*

Okay, she answered immediately. *We're on our way. I
knew you could hear me. Be careful.*

And Elli, I added, *make sure to cover Maiko when you
get here. She's been holding them off outside.*

She's the best guard dog around, Elli assured me. *We'll
take care of her.*

"Why should I let him go, Sebastian?" demanded
Niklas. "I want to be free. I want his gift." He still held me
against the wall, but his grip loosened. "Why should I listen
to you?"

"Because I am your master, Niklas. I allowed you to do
as you please for too long. But no more."

"No more? NO MORE!" Niklas laughed again, but
this time, on top of the usual sadism, there was a hint of
madness. His fingers tightened around my throat again.
He was coming unhinged. "You may have been my master
once, but you are no longer. I am my only master! I will

create a vampire revolution like the world has never seen! Humans will kneel to us. We will be the kings that we were meant to be!"

Sebastian shook his head, unmoving. "You're a fool, Niklas. You have always been a fool. I tolerated your behavior too long, because I love you." Sebastian's voice faltered, and he crossed over to Niklas, reaching out to touch his hair. Although my face was still pushed against the wall, I could see out of the corner of my eye a hint of tenderness wash over Sebastian's brow, and then, almost as quickly, it was gone. "But no more. Your time has come, my love."

"No! I won't let you stop me!" Niklas let go of me, turning on Sebastian and ripping into his neck with his teeth. Sebastian roared with anger and hurled Niklas across the room. Niklas crashed into the sofa and it flipped over on top of him.

I instantly started towards Anastasia, who kicked Katie to the side and struck out to hit me across the face. I slammed back into the wall, pushing off of it to propel my body forward and onto Anastasia, knocking her to the floor. But she *was* stronger than me. She had me flipped over beneath her in a second, pinning me to the floor. She grinned at me.

"Niklas was right. You synthetic-drinkers are weak and pitiful, just like your human girlfrrr—" She stopped short, open-mouthed, her eyes wide. I looked over her shoulder to see Katie breathing hard, her tied-up hands wrapped around one end of a broken chair leg. The other end was buried in Anastasia's back, straight through her heart. I looked back at Anastasia's face, the life fading quickly from her eyes, and rolled her off of me.

"Fuck . . . her," Katie gasped between labored breaths, glaring down disgustedly at Anastasia's lifeless body. "I am *not* weak."

I quickly loosened the rope around her wrists and pulled her behind me, shielding her from the brawl between Sebastian and Niklas. I leaned over and pulled the makeshift spike from Anastasia's back, and, as I caught Sebastian's eye, sent it whizzing through the air towards him. In a fraction of a second, his hand shot out and seized the missile in mid-flight. Then he looked back to Niklas, his face steeling with resolve. In one motion, he spun Niklas's back towards the wall, pinning Niklas's arms and shoulders against it with his left arm, and, with his right arm, shoving the spike just far enough into Niklas's chest to pierce his skin.

Niklas gasped and his eyes, for the first time since I'd known him, widened in fear. "Don't do this," he whispered, his voice quivering. "Don't do it, Seb. I love you."

Sebastian's face melted, but his grip did not. He smiled sadly as a single red tear escaped and rolled down his cheek. "And I love you, my Niki," he whispered, shoving the spike all the way into Niklas's chest. Niklas gasped as his greenish-gray eyes widened, then went completely gray. Sebastian caught his body in his arms, lowering him gently to the floor and leaning down to kiss his cold dead lips. Then he stood and turned to us, blood tears streaming from his dark eyes.

I pulled Katie close to me. "I'm so sorry, Sebastian."

"I loved him, even though he was a monster. He was not always that way." Sebastian sank into the only chair still upright in the room. "When he was a human, he was a good soldier and a caring lover. But when I turned him, he changed. He was never the same again. I never stopped loving him, but I always knew one day I would have to stop him."

"You saved our lives, Sebastian. I know it was not easy for you to kill him, but you're right. He had to be stopped." I put my hand on his shoulder and he placed his hand on mine. "Now we just need to get past all those vampires outside."

"I don't think that will be a problem," he sighed. "I hear Charles and Elli outside now. I think they handled the problem for us."

"But how can you be sure?" Katie asked nervously.

"His hearing is amazing—it surpasses mine by far. It comes with age," I answered. Sebastian looked up at me and smiled sadly.

Evin! Elli's voice rang out in my mind. *Are you okay?*

Yes. We're coming out. I heard Maiko barking excitedly.

"They're waiting for us," I said. Katie and I moved towards the door. "Are you coming, Sebastian?" I turned back to Sebastian, but he had vanished. "Damn. I hate it when he does that."

THE CHOSEN HISTORIAN

ᴄ⁀ Chapter 20 ᴄ⁀

"WHERE is Sebastian? I have a few questions for him," asked Charles, settling into the chair across from me. I was relieved to be back in my own living room after the events of that night.

"I'm not sure. One minute he was there, and the next minute he was gone. I have a feeling we won't be seeing him anytime soon."

"Well, I hope we do. I need answers. All I have is your story and your human girlfriend's, which won't count with the council." Charles adjusted in his seat.

"You know as well as I do what happened, Charles. You

were there for most of it. The council may not listen to Katie, but they will listen to you."

"I was outside the whole time. I can't account for what happened in the house," Charles smirked. "But I'm sure I can figure it out." He got up and moved towards the door, and I followed.

"Thank you, Charles," I said, and I meant it. He may be an arrogant jerk, but he was good at his job. I could never have done it without him, and I was grateful for that. He stopped in the doorway and gave me a smile that actually looked genuine before shutting the door behind him. I wondered what this meant for Charles and me.

"Does this mean he has forgiven you, old chap?" Jakob asked as he entered from the hallway.

"I doubt it, but one can hope. It's at least in a step in the right direction." We headed towards the kitchen, where Elli, Shawn and Katie gathered around the counter.

"So what did Charles say?" Shawn was the first to ask.

"Hey says he will support me, and speak on my behalf to the council." I moved over to Katie and put my arm around her.

"Does this mean you won't be in trouble?" she asked.

"I think I'm in the clear. If you're going to have a vampire on your side, you definitely want it to be Charles." Katie smiled.

"So what next, then?" Jakob asked, but before anyone could answer, his cell phone rang. "Excuse me, I have to take this call," he explained, stepping into the living room.

I answered his question, even though he wasn't there to hear. "Next we go to Ireland to ask the fairies why they were following Noami."

"You promise, Evin?" Elli asked, her voice still shaky from crying. Elli was tough, but what Niklas had told us about our sister had hit her hard.

I reached out to squeeze her hand. "Of course, Elli. We'll find out about Noami's death, and then maybe we'll finally be able to put her soul to rest."

"Well, you won't have to wait long," Jacob answered as he returned to the kitchen. "That was Avery. He has some new information on your sister."

"What is it?" asked Elli.

"She's alive."

"That's not possible!" I exclaimed. "She would be a hundred and sixty-three years old. Unless . . ." I stopped, realizing what this meant. "Oh God, Niklas was lying! He turned her, didn't he?"

Shawn spoke up. "How does Avery know she's alive? If she is a vampire, vampires and fairies don't exactly mix."

Jakob smiled. "She's not a vampire. When Avery went to Seelie Court to inquire further about her they informed him she was okay. He asked how that could be, how she could still be alive. The Queen informed him that Noami was still alive because she is one of them, a fairy."

EVIN DRISCOL SERIES

THE CHOSEN HISTORIAN

Shiba Inu Rescue Association (SIRA) is an all volunteer organization dedicated to saving abandoned, neglected and abused Shiba Inu, Shiba mixes and other primitive breeds from commercial breeders, shelters and owners. SIRA evaluates each dog for temperament and places them in nurturing foster homes where their needs, medical and otherwise, are addressed in order to prepare them to be placed in thoroughly screened, loving, lifelong forever homes. SIRA also works to educate the public on the Shiba Inu breed in addition to the importance of responsible pet ownership including spaying/neutering, dog training and obtaining a dog from a reputable breeder or rescue group.

SIRA does not have a shelter. It is comprised of a network of volunteers and all dogs are fostered in homes. Currently the majority of the volunteers are in Chicago, IL and the surrounding suburbs. SIRA also has volunteers in Southern IL, Indianapolis, IN, Madison, WI, Detroit/Toledo, MI, St. Louis, MO, Phoenix, AZ and South FL. SIRA is constantly expanding so if you are interested in volunteering please read the Help The Shibas pages.

If you would like to make a donation, volunteer, or adopt, you can contact SIRA at **savingshibas.com**. Thank you for your support!

LaVergne, TN USA
03 May 2010
181413LV00001B/123/P